SITHANA BURNING

SOMSY CAMVAN

8th House Publishing
Montreal, Canada

Published worldwide by 8th House Publishing.
Illustrations & Cover Design by 8th House Publishing

ISBN 978-1-926716-74-9

Designed by 8th House Publishing.
www.8thHousePublishing.com
Set in Garamond, Raleway & Grobold.

LIBRARY AND ARCHIVES CANADA CATALOGUING IN PUBLICATION

Title: Sithana burning / Somsy Camvan.
Names: Camvan, Somsy, 1954- author.
Identifiers: Canadiana 20230228445 | ISBN 9781926716749 (softcover)
Classification: LCC PS8605.A567 S58 2023 | DDC C813/.6—dc23

Sithana Burning

I

Toronto, Canada.

LAST WEEK, Sithana became an orphan. A letter from his aunt arrived. "Your mother, father, brother and sister have passed away." He remembered, his aunt is illiterate... Maybe she asked her husband to write the letter.

Later he'd learn: the fire started around one A.M. and burned through the entire house while they slept. The district police were calling it an accident; but all news reporting—from television, newspapers and radio—say it was murder.

His aunt's letter went on to tell him how the bodies of his family were being kept. "We have temporarily buried them in the woods. A proper funeral cannot be held without you. Please come quickly." The letter was dated three months ago. Now, he was in Canada, half a world away, trying to forget the reasons he was forced to escape Laos.

The memories rushed him. He was transported back in time and relived it all in a flash.

✻✻✻✻

Laos. 2 years ago.

A straight-A student at the Lao National University, his parents had been proud of him. They sacrificed themselves to the bone so they could send their son off to university. Then in his second year, Sithana inexplicably joined the anti-government group. Seen at rallies and protests, he was classified a radical and part of the coup that attempted to overthrow the insurgent communist party and reinstall the Royal government. Sithana was only protesting the excessive state control and the abolishment of private property the new government was implementing; but he knew he'd be sentenced to death if arrested and convicted of conspiracy to overthrow the government.

Meanwhile, the police tried to gather evidence. Classmates had been questioned, professors, even cafeterias workers. Everyone knew the leadership of the group met at the university and had its origins among the liberal intellectuals.

One afternoon during a lecture, one of these men burst into the classroom and handed his professor a note. Sithana saw his advisor open the note and read it. A moment later, he stuffed the note into his pocket and looked at the classroom. He had turned the color of ash. His entire body trembled. "The police are here. Class is cancelled. Everyone please go home."

Professor Sinxay looked over to Sithana. They met at the door to the lecture hall.

"There are four police cars in the west parking lot," he told him. "You have to get out of the building quick. Take the emergency exit. Once you get to the first floor, do not run, just walk out the door and slowly to the woods."

The professor put his hand on Sithana's shoulder and looked him in the eyes. "Remember: Straight to the woods! Forget your things. Don't go home. Stay away from the roads and head straight for the shore. Good luck!"

The professor left him standing in the hall realizing that this might be his last day of class forever. He thought of his parents and family. He considered turning himself in again. He remembered what his father had told him. "We know what you are doing. It is a serious crime against the state. You will not get away with it. No one in this organization you are joining, will. For your safety, we ask you to stop. They will take you to the Island, if they find you. You will never get out alive, understand?" Sithana knew what his father meant by the 'Island'. It was the concentration camp in the north for political dissidents.

From the staircase window, Sithana could see policemen with rifles, and military vehicles blocking the entrance to the parking lot. Soldiers came pouring out of them, running out into the front lawn, taking their positions and looking like they were about to face the enemy in a battlefield.

❀❀❀

Thailand. Next day.

SITHANA got to the shore around sunset. He wasted no time and jumped in the river. On the other side was Thailand, but instead of swimming toward it, he let the current take him. It would pull him toward a little bay on the other side. Once ashore, he sat on the sand, back against the dirt embankment. He would remember the warmth of the late afternoon sun as he looked back upon the country he left behind with nothing more than the clothes on his back.

"The path you take in life is your choice," he remembered his grandfather saying. "Don't let anyone tell you what to do." With these words echoing in his memory, Sithana rose to his feet and took to the road. His professor had told him about a refugee encampment at a Buddhist temple further inland.

It was hours before he glimpsed the mango and coconut trees and sandy ground of the temple. He saw no monks, which he thought odd. The UN team had completely taken over the building. They had been originally set up for war refugees, his professor had told him. They were kept active after the war ended in '75 to take in political activists fleeing persecution in Laos.

The next day, his English teacher, an Australian, Mr. John Kenna arrived. Sithana broke down when he saw him. He already felt so alone, but at the same time was suspicious and fearful at the reason for his teacher's presence.

"How did you know I was here?" he asked him.

"Sinxay told me. As a foreigner, I can cross the border freely, in and out of Laos and Thailand. He sent me here to help. We have a plan to help you. You will apply for refugee status. Then you will be protected by the UN. In the meantime, I will send this letter of request to the Australian embassy in Bangkok on your behalf." John held up the letter. "I asked them to consider your case urgent and to get you out of Thailand and into Australia as soon as possible. You must trust me. Stay in the temple and wait. Someone will come to take you to the airport. I assure you."

Australia. A week later.

SITHANA had never left Laos before. He didn't know what to expect of Australia. Upon landing, he noted the weather wasn't much different than Laos. He heard that many countries enjoyed four seasons, but Laos had only three: hot, cold and rainy. He wondered if Australia was the same. A young woman, with short curly brown hair, in a long sleeve shirt and grey jeans was waiting for him outside the plane. He thought, she looked about his age, mid-twenties, standing behind a rope, smiling while holding a sign with his name over her chest.

"I am Sithana."

"Welcome to Sydney. I'm Malisa," she says. "You must be tired. Come, we have a car waiting."

In the car, Malisa had both her hands on the steering wheel, drumming her fingers as if she was enjoying a song in her head. She drove aggressively on the highway, changing lanes to pass other drivers and hardly said a word. Then after the highway exit, stopped at a traffic light, she looked over to him on the passenger seat.

"Have you thought of what you will do, now that you are in Australia?"

"I was in my third-year at university, majoring in

Communication. If I can, I would like to continue my education, maybe even pursue graduate studies. I would like to concentrate on sociology, on culture in particular. I'm a straight-A student."

Sithana fell silent. He didn't know why he had to throw that in. It felt like boasting.

But Malisa didn't dwell on the point. "Why *if?*" she asked.

Sithana shrugged his shoulders. "The education system and language differences."

"I don't think that will be a major barrier. I'm sure if you really want to, you'll make up for any differences as you say."

She smiled at him wistfully. She was an intern social worker at the immigration office sent to pick him up from the airport like many others before him. She thought it was okay if his aim was to eventually pursue a PhD, but the reality that awaited right now was that of a hired hand at a cattle farm.

"You might have known, Laos was not only the poorest country in the world, it was also the most illiterate with seventy-three percent of its population not knowing how to read and write."

She laughed. "You talk like a politician."

Sithana smiled.

"Well… to begin," she went on, "we've found you a

place to stay and work, temporarily. Just to get you on your feet."

"My feet?"

"Up and running."

Sithana looked nonplussed.

"To get you started," Malisa explained. "The most important thing is that you are now safe, fed and sheltered."

"Thank you."

"They are a nice couple… Farming for generations… You'll be staying with them and working on their ranch."

Sithana nodded. "Ranch?"

"Cattle." She looked over at Sithana and saw the blank look on his face. "Cows. Lots of them. It's a beef farm."

"I have never worked on a beef farm before. I used to be afraid of the bull's horns when I was a kid." Sithana looked at her. "But I am not a kid anymore," and turned forward in his seat.

❋❋❋

THE CAMPELLS lived off the main road in a two-storey house. Malisa lead Sithana up to the front door. He could see a herd of cows grazing on the field behind the house. They were all black he noted. Then a flock of black birds flew overhead as Malisa knocked on the door.

Sithana thought they might be omens. "Look at those crows," he says, pointing to the sky.

Malisa looked up. "The ravens, you mean."

"Ah!" he exclaimed, a little embarrassed now at his straight-A student boast, but ultimately relieved.

"Actually, it is easy to confuse the two. They look the same. They say a raven has seven pinion feathers. You know, the big ones at the end of the wing. A crow has sixteen… I think. I'm still not sure myself."

The door opened and middle-aged couple came out to greet them.

Malisa turned to him. "Sithana, this is Kimberly and Robert Campell."

Tall and blonde, the man in overalls, turned his sunburned face at Sithana. He spoke softly, "Hello Sithana," and extended his hand. His wife, slim and dark-haired, twisted into a long braid in the back turned to him smiling.

"I'm sorry, how do you pronounce your name again?"

"Sithana. But you can call me Sith. S-I-T-H."

"I will call you Sithana," she said warmly. "Come inside."

The family home was nothing like what he had imagined it would be when Malisa had told him it was a cattle ranch they were going to. He imagined dusty barns smelling of animal excrement. It was the opposite scene:

all wooden floors, blue antique kitchenette, large living room leather couches and all of it smelling of scented candles.

Kimberly had prepared tea and they were all sipping it. Sithana had never seen such fine porcelain before.

"I am thirty-nine," she was telling him. "Robert is forty-two. We inherited the farm from Robert's family. We both quit school at an early age to work on the land for eighteen years ago. We never had children. The ranch is all we have."

Sithana sat on one of the couches of the living room and noticed how the Campell's darted about. It reminded him of his parents, who to him, also always seemed to be in a hurry. He understood it had something to do with owning land and livestock. There was always too much to do, something else that you need to get to; and the hours never stretch enough. He knew he'd have to adapt, take up that pace again and forego the leisure and long hours he had known at the university as a student. He looked out the living room window and the field, tawny and bronze stretched out in all directions as far as the eye could see. He had not seen such colors in Laos. There the fields were always lush and green. And in the rainy season, the muddied ground held water for months. Fish, frogs and river crabs bred there. They were easy pickings for the farmers who scooped them up and had something besides rice in their fields for a change. Sithana surmised there'd be no such wonders in Australia. He could tell from the Campell's withered faces and tired eyes that life here was harsh and the river never visited their fields with such gifts.

✳✳✳✳

SITHANA rose the next morning to find the Campell's already awake. He could hear Kimberly downstairs in the kitchen.

"I've prepared breakfast," she said. "Coffee?" she asked, handing him a cup.

"I am sorry, I woke up so late. I wasn't too sure of the schedule here."

"Not to worry. We want you to feel at home. Robert is with a neighbour helping another neighbour with his field. You'll see, we help each other a lot here. We need to… It will take you a couple of day to get used to our routine. I'll show you around once you're done with breakfast. Come get me in the shed."

Sithana looked down at his plate. He had never seen such strange food before.

KIMBERLY was giving Sithana the tour of the ranch. Their German shepherd had decided to accompany them on their walk. He ran ahead of them all the while, leaping through the tall grass, then stopping and waiting for them when he got too far ahead.

"You have a very smart dog," Sithana said.

Kimberly smiled. "We got him when he was only eight weeks old. He's four, almost five now. Robert sure does loves him. And of course, so do I... Did you have a dog back home?"

"We have three dogs, but we never let them in the house. They aren't trained like Cloy. We keep them mostly for protection. Their furs are not so nice. They are short, rough and red."

"We have dogs of that color here. Dingos, we call them. But they are wild and we shoot them if they come too close. They'll attack the herd in packs and slaughter as much they can. This is why we built this fence around the land," Kimberly said, showing him the last corner post of the fence that she had taken him to. "This is the edge of our land. Everything from here is ours."

Sithana nodded that he understood. He was struck at the vastness of their land. His parents' rice patty farm wasn't a tenth of this, but had enough room to grow food for the whole family and make a living selling the rest at market. It wasn't only the size of the land, but the assortment of tools, the fat on the animals, the bed he slept in, the furniture… and the home was so much more comfortable. The barn itself was of better construction than the home of the richest man in their village.

"In total, we have seven hundred hectares," Kimberly added.

"I can't imagine," he said, still awestruck. "You must be very wealthy. In Laos, you would be the richest family."

She smiled. "We are not rich. There are much bigger ranches than ours. I don't know much, I dare say, but I imagine it's easier to farm in Laos or Thailand. Much greener there…But here the land is hard and dry and there isn't much growth. We need a lot of area or the animals won't have enough to grange."

Sithana returned her smile. "You and your husband are lucky."

"Yes, we feel lucky to be able to live off our land and herd. But it's hard work. That's why we need you…"

They sat down to lunch that day and everyone was curious about Sithana and why he had fled Laos. They kept shaking their heads as he told him his story and Sithana felt how sympathetic they were when even most people back home, would simply shrug it off as another fact of life.

"It is everyday life for many people in Laos. It is maybe, nothing."

Robert was amazed. "It isn't *nothing*. You were arrested."

"Only once," Sithana said.

"Well… you are very brave," Kimberly added.

"After the liberation in 1975, Laos became communist. The neighboring countries, Vietnam, China and Cambodia were already communist so Laos had no choice."

"Laos is a landlocked country," Robert explained to his wife. "It is surrounded by these communist neighbours."

"Yes, Laos needs a great deal of support from other countries," Sithana went on. "Everyone in the region is poor, and all the aid comes from Russia. But with that support comes political and economic control. Since Laos became a communist regime, we have lost most of our rights. Even freedom of speech. Revolt began at the universities. A movement for the "freedom of expression" began."

Kimberly and Robert looked at each other and shook their heads again. "This is when they arrested you?" Robert asked.

"All we wanted was to encourage students to debate certain issues. We organized and wrote government officials requested that they release the innocent they had sent to labor camps. We requested that they stop arresting those who denounced the government and we protested against the curfews and martial law they imposed. The movement spread through the whole country."

Robert looked at Sithana earnestly. "Well, at least here in Australia you can say what you want about the stinking government! Bunch of louts!"

Kimberly shook her head. "Oh, Robert!"

Robert and Kim let out a laugh, so Sithana laughed also.

"We're happy to sponsor you and do our little bit for freedom in Laos," Robert concluded. "After lunch, if you think you might be ready, I'd like to show you around the barn and some of the chores we need you to do."

At that moment a grasshopper alighted on the table. Kimberly gasped.

"Oh! It must have come in through the window. Nasty critters! It's from all the tall grass we have in the field this time of year. I hope you weren't frightened," she said turning to Sithana.

Sithana smiled. "In Laos, we eat them."

❆❆❆❆

SITHANA had been at the Campell's for months now. He often thought of his studies and began fearing that if he didn't enroll soon, he might find himself stuck in this situation as a refugee cattle farmer the rest of his life. He didn't care that he was being paid and seeing more money in his pocket than he had known his whole life. He had begun fretting about his age, about being away from school for too long and soon all he could think about was how his dream of a PhD was slipping away. He knew he had to focus on returning to his university studies. He would need money to live and study in the city. He'd have to move from the farm. Even if he remained here somehow, he'd have little time to read. It wasn't exactly a literary house. The only reading materials he had ever found were some old equine magazines about best breeding practices, littered with ads on where to find studs and their fees. Sithana found it odd that Australians would pay for males to impregnate the females. He knew the Campell's did the same and often sought bulls from as far away as possible. It was healthy, they told him.

It's true he was learning a lot, not only from his ranch work, but from conversing with Robert and Kimberly. He felt indebted to them, and to the immigration officer and staff for all their help, but knew he had to move on.

Robert and Kimberly were fond of him. He had been a good helper. Even though a bigger, stronger man would have been better for the job, he did as he was told and worked hard. It took him awhile at first to get used to everything. They gave him overalls to wear, but they were much too big. "You wear them over your regular clothes,"

Kimberly said. So he tried them on over his other clothes, but they were still too big. The straps get falling off his shoulders. Finally, he took a rope and tied it around his waist to keep the overalls up. It was around that time that he first met Laura, the Hammond's daughter from the neighbouring ranch. A student at Sydney University, she came home for weekends and holidays only. Tall, slim, blue-eyed and with curly dark hair—Sithana had never seen a woman like that in his life. All the girls back home had the same straight hair and color eyes. Sithana began spending as much time with her as he could. He fantasized about running off with her to university. It was all the more reason to push forward with his studies. He could never be with Laura if all he was, was a refugee cattle prodder.

When the time came to make the decision; it was doubly hard. Sinxay had written him via the immigration office. He had a colleague in Canada, he wrote. He had fled Laos and was now teaching at a university there. He would help Sithana get settled and enrolled at the university, but it meant leaving not only the Campells, but Laura also.

❈❈❈

Toronto, Canada. About a year and a half later.

SITHANA had worked hard all day at the office. The boss had been kind and asked if he was tired after seeing he wasn't in the mood to talk. He often thought of home, of his parents and his sister. It's not that he was tired; he had begun to question whether he would ever see them again. Ever since he arrived in Canada, the world he once knew seemed further from him than ever. From six to seven every evening, regularly like clockwork, he'd sit down and listen to the VAO radio that broadcasted Laotian news. He had been eager that very same day to get home for the daily dose of radio new updates, but instead got it via letter. It was from his aunt Bouy and it would change his life forever.

SITHANA went in to work early the next day. He had made up his mind. Leena, a coworker saw him loitering by the entrance.

"You're here early," she said, and then saw the look on his face. "Is everything alright?"

"I just received a letter," he told her. "From three months ago! My family... they are all dead."

Leena looked into his eyes. "Oh my! That's horrible!

All of them? What happened?"

Sithana looked away. "A fire," they say. "But I don't know…"

She put a hand on his shoulder. "I'm so sorry for your loss, let me know if I can help in anyway." Sithana nodded, fighting back the tears.

"Three months ago…God, I can't imagine how you must be feeling. What are you going to do?"

"I don't know… but I will return to Laos to find out what's really happened. I need to talk to our boss about time off."

"Of course… He'll understand."

SITHANA'S boss was understanding just as Leena said he'd be. "Take all the time you need," he suggested. "Your job will be waiting for you when you get back."

He wasn't quite sure how many hours the flight from Canada to Laos would take. It was all too confusing with all the hour changes and connections all the way. First, was the departure from Toronto's Pearson international airport, Toronto to London's Heathrow airport. From there he would connect to a flight to Bangkok, and from Thailand, a local Thai airline to Vientiane, Laos.

He imagined that most passengers on board from North America were about to go to southeast Asia for vacation and adventure. Their faces betrayed that excitement and exhilaration. Sithana guessed they knew nothing of the war there, nor the human rights violations and all the atrocities their citizens endured every day. Nor could they imagine that, in their very midst, was a Laotian who was living evidence of it all—exiled, and now returning home under secrecy to attend to his family's death, whom may have all been murdered.

Vientiane - Luang Prabang, Laos. Present day.

ARRIVING at the international airport in Vientiane, he collected his bags and headed for the bus terminal. He recalled his home village where his aunt still lived in the Laung Prabang province, vividly. He should be there in the morning if he managed to catch the 6pm bus. He was fearful and afraid, like in the old days. He had to remind himself that with a Canadian passport and his new Canadian identity, they wouldn't attempt anything even if they recognized him.

The Luang Prabang bus station was in the center of the city. It was crowded as always, with mostly domestic passengers. The building itself was made of cement poles, high ceilings, tin roofs, a dirt, gravel floor. It was built in a loop; with shops and stands overlooking the arrival and departure areas. He ate at one of the stands in the loop, forgetting how good the food was, before taking a rickshaw to the Mekong to catch a ferry to cross the river.

It was some eight kilometres from the shore to the village by ferry, and perhaps it was the rushing water beneath the boat, or the crossing of the river' but it seemed like it was suddenly all 'hitting home' and coming to life for him. Until now, receiving the letter, boarding the planes—it had all seemed like a dream. Now, he was firmly cemented on his feet, aware of them perhaps because of the lolling deck beneath them, and the facts assailed him. Burned alive? Was it, could it have been, deliberate? Anger swelled inside him.

His aunt's house, as he remembered it, was on a narrow path that passed through the center of the village and lead to the main dust road that snaked up the hill and lead out of the village. The path would be too narrow for any driver, so Sithana had to walk the way.

Approaching the spot where he thought his aunt's house should be, he was no longer sure. The streets had changed; the houses, too. Some had been repainted, others renovated or replaced completely. He looks them over one by one until he comes to one in particular, made of wooden sideboard. Around it are bushes and shrubs, outlined with red gravel. The plants are old, some decaying; but the house looks as if it was built yesterday.

He appeared to be lost in a trance, trying to merge the memory of his aunt's house with what lay before him. He couldn't be sure. He made no movement, when two dogs came out, barking, sniffing at his shoes. He barely noticed the middle-aged woman who had opened the door and was now standing there in tears, looking at him.

"We have been waiting for you…" his aunt said.

She walked over. Sithana dropped his suitcase and hugged her as she cried on his shoulder. Then she laid her palms on each side of his cheeks.

"You are taller and fatter, now my boy Sithana! Come in."

They stepped inside and Buoy noticed Sithana taking in the changes.

"We rebuilt the house after…. You know… the fire… Everything is completely new," she suddenly broke out, elated. "Even the stove. And we just finished installing the siding last week."

Sithana couldn't help but notice that there were no pictures or portraits of the family anywhere to be seen.

"Yes, big change," Sithana remarked.

Stepping out into the hall was his uncle Ken. He walked over to Sithana with his hand extended. "Welcome back son," he mouthed, without a smile and without any warmth.

The bad act wasn't lost on Sithana and it made him wonder. He reached into his bag and pulled out a souvenir t-shirt. "From Canada," Sithana said, handing it to his uncle, who took it with a crooked smile.

His uncle pat him on the back. Again, Sithana couldn't help but notice the affectation. "I'll leave you with your aunt. I'll be back later," he said and left.

"You must be tired," his aunt suggested. "I'll show you to your bedroom. I'll start preparing supper soon. You can rest until then."

Bouy lead him to the bedroom and Sithana noticed again the conspicuous absence of any family photos. There had been so much history here. He was born in this house for one. He found it odd. Even if all the photos had been destroyed in the fire…Surely his aunt had pictures of her own she could've hung on the walls.

❊❊❊

AUNT BOUY was in the kitchen preparing supper. Sithana was sitting outside on the front porch watching the children playing on the street, spinning and chasing after an old bicycle tire. It was past five o'clock and the village was under shade. He was trying to process all he had learned and seen since his arrival. His uncle Ken's behavior particularly perplexed him. He was sure something was wrong and he had made up his mind to confront him. He was pondering the best way of going about that when a woman walked up to him, smiling.

"You don't remember me?" she asked him

"You look different," he answered at once, recognizing Viengvilay, his sister's old friend.

They had known each other since they were children and played together in the streets like the children were playing now. Sithana hadn't seen her since he was fifteen when he left to pursue his studies in the capital Vientiane. She had remained good friends with his little sister Dara. Now that Sithana was seeing her for the first time as an adult, he was stricken by her beauty; but more so by her kindness and the attention she showed him. He hadn't been with her very long, but he was already smitten. His priority though was to garner information on what had happened to his family and in that moment, he buried the attraction he felt for her, for the sake of hearing what she might have to say.

"So you and Dara were good friends…"

She made no motion, but smiled sadly.

Looking at her he was again taken in by her beauty. He looked away. "I remember my sister mentioned you often in her letters."

Viengvilay blushed and looked to the ground. "Actually…"

Sithana thought this might be the moment. "Actually what?"

"We were writing them together."

Sithana relaxed in his seat. "I miss her."

"I miss her too," Viengvilay confessed and began sobbing.

Sithana observed her closely and was convinced there was something she wanted to tell him. He decided not to press her, feeling confident she would tell him on her own terms and at her own time.

Then his aunt interrupted them. She had been poking her head in and out of the door on occasion all this time—to spy on them, Sithana thought, as all old women in the village felt it was their prerogative to do whenever a young unmarried woman was involved..

"Why don't you two come in and sit inside," his aunt Buoy suggested, and then turning to Viengvilay: "Won't you stay for supper? We must celebrate Sithana's return even if it is a sad occasion."

Viengvilay graciously accepted to stay for supper. She had been looking forward to Sithana's arrival ever since she heard he was returning. She had fallen in love with him long before he had left for university. Then more and more time passed and she heard he had fled the country. Viengvilay gave up hope and resigned herself to the life of a spinster. She remained in her parents' home, and taught elementary school—at the very same school she and Sithana had attended.

She knew he had been living in Canada, a modern, industrialized nation. Now, she feared that he had outgrown his Laotian ways and would find her unattractive.

Sithana for his part, couldn't understand why she was

so fond of him and why his aunt encouraged her presence. Despite himself, he was smitten by her every gesture and word at supper, but still didn't fail to notice again, his uncle's reticence and nervous behavior. He avoided looking up from his plate it seemed to Sithana, and hardly said a word. Then every time, Dara's name was mentioned, his uncle appeared uneasy.

Now after dinner, Viengvilay and Sithana were walking through the village, taking in the air and letting their stomachs settle.

"We all remember the day you left," Viengvilay said, looking into his eyes. "It was so sudden."

"I had no choice," Sithana answered.

"Pff!" Viengvilay teased. "You just got tired of rice and bamboo shoots."

"Rice and bamboo shoots?"

"It's the only thing we eat here, remember?"

Sithana laughed, and couldn't help but notice how she was able to put him at ease so effortlessly. "Did you know I was coming?" he asked.

Viengvilay nodded. "Your aunt told me. She asked if I would keep you company."

"She did? And what did you answer."

Viengvilay looked down, smiling. "I told her, I would be happy to."

"What does my uncle Ken think about that?"

"I don't know…He never says anything…only listens."

"He is good man," Sithana ventured.

Viengvilay made no response, which added to the growing suspicion Sithana had of his uncle. They continued walking in silence. Sithana felt that she wasn't quite the girl he remembered as being reserved and quiet. Now she was outspoken, expressing her thoughts and opinions openly on politics and the government and most importantly on his family situation which she knew so much about—possibly more than he since he'd been away. Most importantly, she seemed genuinely concerned. She had even promised to give him an article written about the incident that she had kept. She was convinced like the others, that it has been no accident and that his family was murdered. She tells him she doesn't believe the police investigation, not for a minute.

"Sometimes they arrest innocent men for a crime," she told him, "and then kill them in jail to cover up letting the guilty ones go free."

These were things Sithana was well aware of. "What can we do to bring those responsible to justice then?"

"We must do all we can or it will never stop. We have to try at least," she answered.

"You are very kind," Sithana said. "I was thinking the same thing." He stopped and hugged her.

Behind them, a man who had been following them

and trying as best as he could to eavesdrop on their conversation, stepped behind a tree to conceal himself after he noticed they had stopped to embrace.

Sithana and Viengvilay were oblivious, lost in each other's company. Darkness had descended upon the village along with a cool breeze that blew in softly. Fireflies everywhere filled the air with twinkling lights.

SITHANA was standing on the porch of his aunt's house waving to Viengvilay after she parted from him to return to her home. A feeling of loneliness descended upon him. With his family gone, he felt like everything was slipping away. Even the town had changed. And this very house, his aunt and uncle were living in now was only a small hut back when Sithana lived there as a boy. In those days, the Village was about ninety huts set about haphazardly on the uneven ground in the middle of the jungle forest. Now nearly all the huts were gone, replaced by cement homes. Even the sloping ground and mounds had been flattened. The only huts to be seen now were along the edge of the village. One could tell their age from the color of their palm leaf roofs. They aged from green to golden.

Money brought in the gangsters and criminals after the government began allowing from private businesses to operate. Many villages, like Sithana's became centers of government corruption with officials running around illegally buying and selling lands, assisting drug-trafficking, selling logging contracts and even recruiting for prostitution. The government appropriated land wherever they chose and threatened and even murdered those who refused to sell. Younger families were more open to relocating and moving into these new cement homes, but many of the older generation were not. They began disappearing. People in the village, especially farmers felt like they were living the war all over again and in order to survive, had to turn a blind eye and endure the violence and injustice. Most of the businesses were shell companies created expressly for the purpose of embezzling government funds and foreign aid.

Viengvilay turned a corner and disappeared down the road from his sight. Now, he felt truly alone. He would have to face great dangers soon, and there was so very little time to do it all: relocate his family's remains for a proper burial, dealing with the federal police and trying to bring the killers to justice. He remembered Viengvilay's offer to help. "I am lucky to have her on my side," he thought as he re-entered the house.

Again it struck him: no family photos on the walls... He went for his bags in his room and took out some of the gifts he had brought for his aunt and uncle. Among these were photos he had brought for the service and memorial they would hold.

"This is for you," he said, handing his aunt the gift. "It is from Canada. Sweet, gold water from a tree. It is called *maple syrup.*"

"Oh Sithana! Thank you! Look Ken," she said, turning to his uncle. "Look what Sithana brought us!"

"I also have this…" Sithana added, holding the photo up in his hands to look at it. "I'm not sure if you're in this photo," he told his aunt Bouy.

"Let me see it."

His aunt took up the photo to examine it.

"I noticed you have no photos of the family on the walls," Sithana now mentioned. "You can keep that one."

Ken, at the kitchen, cleared his throat, stood up and walked out the door.

IT HAD been a long day for Sithana. He was tired, but too many thoughts ran through his head as he lay in bed. He couldn't get the images of his family's faces out of his mind. Old memories flooded him. He remembered a chilly September in 2005, when his mother had accompanied him to the bus station when he was off to university for the first time. He recalled his excitement at leaving for Vientiane the capital city, where he would complete his high school and enroll in university. He heard his mother's voice again, pledging him to return home after completing his studies and take an important role in the tribe, to work for the tribal community and make them proud. He realized now that this must be every parents' wish for their children. It was the last time he would see his mother. And that morning, before they left for the bus station—when his father, brother and little sister stood at the door waving him goodbye—that would be the last time he saw *them* alive. Sithana's eyes welled up with tears, but a rage was also rising within him. What he was about to do was throw himself into a fire pit. If the flames were low enough, he might survive and crawl out; but if the flames were too high, they would engulf him and he'd be burned to death. Was it worth risking his own life to bring the perpetrators to justice?

Sithana tossed and turned until his mind brought him to the memory of his time with Viengvilay that afternoon. Suddenly, he felt content and drifted off to sleep.

❈❈❈❈

SITHANA was eager to get started and brought up the remains while sitting down to breakfast with his aunt Bouy and uncle Ken the next morning. His aunt was suggesting they could go whenever Sithana pleased when his uncle interrupted her, "We will have to make the arrangements first."

"Yes, of course... But he may want to visit them beforehand. I know I would..." she went on. "And you know, Sithana, if you wanted to stay longer... I mean you can stay as long as you like... if you wanted to... You could live with us for as long as you like."

"Sithana is better off living where he was," Ken interjected. "He's a man now and he needs to find his own way."

"Yes, of course..." his aunt conceded. "But all the same, it will take some time for all this business to—"

Ken grunted. He knew that Sithana had to resolve the issues with the remains and the business of the inheritance, but he felt the boy was asking for trouble the longer he stayed and the more he poked around. He turned to his wife and Sithana, "The old ones used to say, before you sit on a cushion of thick leaves, check the leaves first. There might be a snake hiding there."

His aunt shrugged her shoulders as if dismissing the admonition. "So... Sithana, what will you be doing today?"

"I am meeting Viengvilay. She has offered to help," Sithana answered.

"I think you should make your own decisions, son," Ken interjected.

"Yes. But I need more information from her."

Ken looked nervous suddenly. He leaned back in his chair. "I just want you to know... I think Bouy should have told you, that Viengvilay is engaged." He leaned forward at the table again and picked up his fork. "To the son of a very powerful man. So, I want you to be careful with her."

His aunt scoffed. "The boy knows who he is talking to!"

THE SCHOOL Viengvilay was teaching at was at a corner of the village, about half a kilometer from Sithana's aunt's house. His uncle knew a shortcut which he offered to show, but Sithana said he'd would go off alone and reacquaint himself with the village to which his uncle grunted in response. Sithana was glad he had come alone. He was not so sure that Viengvilay would have spoken so freely had his uncle been there. They were sitting in a park by the school, far from anyone's earshot.

"I'm tired of seeing all this crime and dirty business in our villages my whole life. This place is a mess. We need someone to speak up or at least make the criminals known to the federal authorities," Viengvilay was saying.

Sithana looked her in the eyes. She wasn't as soft or deferent as she had been yesterday. Her mood had changed to something imperious, firm and forceful. She seemed more determined than Sithana who still had his doubts.

"It won't be me to speak up; I'm a foreigner now," he reminds her.

"It doesn't have to be you...But you've hardly changed, you know, and you haven't forgotten a word of our language." she added. "But, I understand."

They're both aware of the consequences of taking action on their own anger. In his case, his name would be sure to appear on a list for immediate deportation and without possibility of return. They would ban him from Laos forever. That was only if they were fortunate not to 'disappear' as so many have.

Viengvilay asked Sithana to supper at her place that night. They would make a decision on how to bring the family's remains back from the woods, to the village cemetery and have the remains properly buried. On his way home, Sithana tried to make sense of all he had learned. Of course, he had already imagined when he received the news that there deaths had been the result of a land dispute. The first thing he learned was that the fire had been caused by a bomb. The second was that it hadn't been the first bomb or attempt on their life. A week before they were killed, another bomb had exploded in the rice field where they were having lunch. They survived the first incident without a scratch. Perhaps they thought it was a mine left over from the war that had exploded accidentally. These things were known to happen, but not in this part of Laos. In fact that rice field, their entire village even, had been somewhat sheltered from the war. The two armies never met anywhere in the vicinity and no bombs or other munitions left over had ever been found in the area.

SITHANA arrived at Viengvilay's home a few minutes before supper. Wooden stairs led to a typical house of the region, eight steps above ground with a sizable enough awning for keeping livestock such as cows or buffalos. Sithana however saw no animals or evidence that any had been kept recently; and once he entered the house, he wondered if aanyone was home at all.

"Good," she exclaimed upon seeing him. "You came early…Do you want to help me set supper?"

Sithana agreed and turned to find the table. He had been living in the west for far too long and it took him some time to realize that Viengvilay was still living traditionally and eating on mats on the floor. Sithana lay the first trays by the cushions.

They sat on the floor facing each other and began

eating. Sithana observed her keenly, never imagining the girl he knew twenty year ago would become this beautiful, tall, slim woman with luscious black hair. He was smitten once more by her beauty.

"Now, I suppose you can tell me everything?" Sithana said, looking her in the eyes waiting for her answer.

"What do you mean?"

"I feel like you haven't told me everything you know."

"No, not everything," she admitted.

"Tell me," he said. "Don't be afraid."

"You know that our families were close…" she said and began blushing slightly. "I think your mother was hoping that you and I might… you know…. That the families would be united. Your father too. They always stopped in the street to talk me and I visited them and Dara often. I was there when it began. You know your father's strong character… Well, they tried a number of times. But he wouldn't accept the price, wouldn't accept any price they had to offer, he said. So they sent him a check and bundled it with it a threat. He had twenty-four hours to sign."

Sithana nodded. "I see…My father should have known better," Sithana said.

At that moment, Viengvilay broke down and started crying. "We should all know better!"

Sithana leaned in to comfort her.

"You don't know," she confessed. "I'm engaged to—"

"Yes, my uncle told me."

"No! You don't understand. I should have known better myself…"

Sithana was not following. "I don't understand," he admitted. "You don't love him?"

She looked up at him and spoke softly, wiping away the tears. "It's not just that…He's the son… you know… He belongs to people, the sort of people that may have done this. I'm so sorry!"

Sithana took her in his arms. "It's not your fault. But if you don't love him, why marry him?"

"Oh Sithana! Don't you understand anything? It isn't safe. Not for you, not for me," she said and broke down sobbing again. "They should all be rounded up and put to work growing rice… I hate them!" she exclaimed and then looked up to meet Sithana's eyes. "You believe me, don't you?"

"Yes, Viengvilay, I believe you."

Sithana felt the attraction he held for her mounting within him. He felt that if he was ever going to kiss her, this would be the time, but the moment he made the decision, she turned away and appeared destitute looking at the floor. Moments later, she was up on her feet.

"I have some mangos for dessert," she said, wiping her eyes and trying to muster some cheer. "They're from the back yard. You won't get mangos like these in Canada!"

She went to the kitchen and reappeared with the fruit.

VIENGVILAY had agreed to help him. She had even taken time off her teaching schedule so she could do so. Now, on his way home, Sithana was asking himself if all this was rational, if he was behaving responsibly. He knew the dangers—everyone did—and that they had warned him repeatedly. Now, here he was putting Viengvilay at risk also.

Before he left her, she had mentioned taking time off again so she could help him. "You don't mind?" he asked her.

She looked him in the eyes. "Well then, I would like to cover the ten days for you," Sithana suggested.

"Yes, I mind," she answered and then added, "You don't need to worry about covering my pay, you can buy me a stone later," she said, smiling and pointing at her finger.

Now he was thinking that perhaps he shouldn't see her again. She was engaged after all. Besides their poking around on the activities of these poachers, he was now flirting with a woman engaged ostensibly to a very dangerous man. If he were wise, he thought, he would just visit with his aunt while he was here, have her bring him to the cemetery, recite prayers for his family and return to the airport as quickly as possible. But when he thought of the bus ride from Luang Prabang to the Vientiane airport his resolve began to waver. He knew, as he had experienced on his way to the village only days ago, that the ride would be a tribulation. All these buses looked and operated in the same way: No windows that opened, younger men travelling on the roof of the bus, others hanging off its sides; passengers within swearing, talking loudly, complaining of discomfort until they were too sick to do so, vomiting all over the bus because the road was in such poor condition, unpaved, snaking up and down the hills of the high mountains with all of them jostling within its tin can—and all for a good nine to fourteen hours depending on the weather and other circumstances. The worst of it would be that he would return home without ever having learned the truth about his family's death. He knew his resolve would falter on the bus ride alone, and that once back in Canada, he wouldn't be able to forgive himself or put the matter to rest. He decided to stay and this decision seemed to put him at peace. Despite the risks, he knew now that he had no real choice. If he had the opportunity to flee, he wouldn't take it.

THE following day Viengvilay took Sithana to see his family's gravesite, about five minutes' walk from the village. The villagers didn't want them in the cemetery as their death was from unnatural causes. The superstition was that an untimely death was a curse, and that this curse like all curses spreads from person to person, house to house, village to village, even after one is dead. Sithana knew that it had been his aunt's wish to have them buried in that place at the village's border; but he hadn't heard the whole story until now.

"At first the village chief wanted them to be sent to the old village where both your parents were born," Viengvilay recounted. "But your aunt told him that they had no relatives living there....So they agreed to bury them here. A week later, your aunt paid the chief to place the deed of your parents' house in her name, explaining that you were living abroad and that she needed the deed so she could make reparations after the fire. I think maybe your uncle made her do it."

"He used to work in a police station...I don't know what happened to him, he stopped working before the age of retirement."

It was a hot day with the sun glaring down on them as they trekked toward the cemetery. Once in the woods, the heavy foliage cut the faint breeze that was blowing. The air grew heavy and humid. Viengvilay stopped to take off her long sleeve shirt. Sithana watched as the outline of her breasts and the rise of her nipples poked through the thin white cotton of her undershirt.

"Aren't you hot?" she said looking at his thick jeans and heavy, cotton shirt.

But when it became apparent that Sithana had no intention of removing any layer of clothing, she retorted. "I wonder, if foreigners are afraid of the insects here."

"They might be," Sithana replied. "But I'm not." Then for some reason he could not explain, he blundered, adding, "I am keeping my long shirt on out of respect for the spirits of my family," just as Viengvilay was tying the shirt she had just taken off, around her waist. Sithana had lost his faith in these superstitions long ago. He believed himself an atheist in fact. He had no reason to say such a thing and he knew it.

Viengvilay apologized.

"Forget I said that...I was only kidding," was all Sithana could think of saying.

Viengvilay pushed on ahead of him, leading the way. "Watch out for stones, "she reminded him. "They can be slippery!"

Sithana recalled her remark about buying her a stone.

They crept down the river bank, holding on to branches and each other to keep from falling into the ditch below.

"I've been thinking about you," Sithana confessed.

They both stopped. Sithana could hear the shallow, rippling water of the creek below as its clear waters ran over the mossy, brown rocks. It seemed to him that it had a form of music all its own.

"There!" Viengvilay said, pointing to a spot across the bank where the earth next to a copse seemed recently disturbed. Sithana saw four distinct mounds.

SITHANA and Viengvilay were sitting on an outcropping of rock adjacent to the burial site.

"Thank you for doing this for me," Sithana said. "I really do appreciate it. I would be lost without you. I know my aunt and uncle have good intentions, but they don't seem willing to help. They must be afraid of the consequences."

"I'm not only doing it for you," Viengvilay told him. "I am doing this for myself as well, you know." She looked him in the eyes. "Your family have always been so kind to me. Your father especially. He used to say, that he was planning a big…" Viengvilay blushed. "…wedding for us when you returned from university, but then…"

"But then I had to leave the country," Sithana interjected.

"We never got to see you graduate," Viengvilay continued. "Then on my graduation day, I remember.

Your mother… I was so shy, I didn't want to go to the event. Your mother, she came to our house. She brought a graduation gift for me she said. It was a beautiful dress to wear the day of the ceremony. If it wasn't for her… I would never have known what it was like to feel proud of myself and see that same feeling in my family's eyes."

"I'm sorry I wasn't there," Sithana said. "I would have been proud too. People kept promising me that I would be able to return home soon."

"They told us that you had left for Australia…But then you went to Canada."

"I wanted to finish my studies…"

"Do you remember that day before you left? It was monsoon season and we all went out in the rain. The rain was pouring down as if the sky had opened up. I got a chill and began sneezing. Everyone wanted to go down to the river to swim. You told me to go home, that if I got sick and died, it would be my own fault. It made me think you didn't care."

"I remember. You went home…"

"It was the last time I saw you."

Viengvilay said this and rose. Sithana watched in confusion as she crossed the creek before getting up to follow her.

They walked in silence for awhile and then Sithana spoke: "So…where is the lucky man from? Your fiancé…"

"From Luang Prabang City," she answered. "Why?"

Sithana could see that she was on the verge of tears. "I am sorry if I made you feel uncomfortable," he said.

She looked down. "What have you been doing there all this time?" she asked. "In Canada I mean…"

But before Sithana could answer, she had sped off down the path again. Some steps later, without breaking her stride, she asked, "Do you have someone in your life there? I'm sure you have."

It was a difficult question for him to answer. He did have someone, possibly, in Canada…but certainly he didn't have feelings for her like he was having now for Viengvilay. He had not expected this, and wasn't sure what to do about it. She was engaged after all…And he had never thought of her in this way. She had been that scrawny childhood friend of his sister and nothing more. What was he to do about this now?

They reached the village and crossing the main passage, came across a group of men chatting who fell silent as they walked by. The chatter resumed once Sithana and Viengvilay were some paces away, with snickering and laughter. Sithana and Viengvilay looked at each other.

"I'd better not stop," Viengvilay said.

"I'll walk you home," Sithana suggested.

They hadn't taken but a half-dozen paces when a village boy came running up to them.

"Teacher! Teacher!" he cried, bringing up his hand to shield his eyes from the sun's glare. "The police are looking for you and your friend."

Viengvilay and Sithana looked at each other.

"Where are they now?" Viengvilay asked.

"They're all over the village. Two of them are at your house," the boy replied. "The others are looking for him," he said, pointing at Sithana.

Sithana and Viengvilay watched as the boy changed direction and ran down another path. "You should hide," Viengvilay told Sithana. "It's not safe."

"What about you?"

"I have to go home. The police won't bother me. They know I'm Touy's fiancée. It's you they're looking for… They'll know you've been staying at your uncle's. Better go to the edge of the field. You'll see an abandoned shack. Wait there until sunset; the police would have gone by then. I'll try and get you before then, if it's safe."

Sithana watched as Viengvilay ran off home. He set off in the opposite direction but then looked back again— she was already hidden behind the bamboo, not looking back at him. As Sithana walked towards the abandoned shack, he felt the heat of the sun on his back as he darted from building to building until he reached the fields. In the full glare of the afternoon sun, everything seemed lifeless, with only the banana leaves moving in the breeze.

Sithana darted towards the shack that Viengvilay told him about. When he arrived at the abandoned hut, he climbed up and sat leaning against a pole, worrying about Viengvilay and thinking about what he should do. He wasn't even a citizen of this country anymore. He thought about contacting the Canadian consulate in Vientiane. But his case wasn't politically relevant and he might face prejudiced sentiments from individual diplomats. As Sithana looked out at the empty fields, he felt a mix of fear, anger, and excitement. Then as the sun began to set and Viengvilay still hadn't appeared, he began to wonder if he would ever see her again.

❈❈❈❈

HIS UNCLE Ken was waiting at the front door for him. Sithana recognized his suitcase laying at his uncle's feet.

"You've been here a couple of days only and already have brought us trouble."

Sithana tried to protest. "Uncle, I've done nothing. I've—"

"The police have been here…asking us—your aunt—all manner of questions about you. You know her heart condition… And you've done nothing? You think they have nothing better to do than to come here to pass the afternoon?" He shook his head. "You and that Viengvilay—I told your aunt she was trouble. I always knew it."

"She is innocent, uncle! She has done nothing. She only wants to help."

"Help! Ha! You've been poking about in police business. You go to a foreign country and now you think you know better than everyone? Let the police do their job, yes?" His uncle seemed to soften. "Listen son. You're a grown man now... Take my advice: Bury your parents and go back to Canada before you make too many problems for yourself and you never get to see those white girls again..." His uncle looked him in the eyes. "You understand me?" He handed him the suitcase. "Now go. You can't stay here anymore. The police will be back, looking for you. Your aunt is already sick with nerves."

I I I

LUANG PRABANG, the capital city, had a somewhat Parisian appearance. The old royal palace, set in the heart of the city, is surrounded by old traditional style housing, as well as large and taller French-style buildings dating as far back as 1893 when the French took Laos as its protectorate to protect against Thai invasions. After the French left Indochina in 1954, the city experienced a brief period of independence. People were proud to have their own government and military units rather than relying on French protection, which had been a source of colonial resentment for a long time. However, the country was soon faced with another war, this time to defend the city from a Communist takeover. The royal army was supported by the United States. However, when the country and the city fell to the Communists in 1975, the royal family disappeared and the palace was turned into a museum. The new transitional government was no better than the previous French or CIA secret war periods, and the behavior of the new elites was often horrific as they used their inherited tyrannical ideologies to harm those who defied them. This behavior was largely ignored by the international community and human rights groups, so there was no pressure on the government or new elites, many of whom turned to organized crime.

After the Communists took over the country, the new elites bred under communist rule were proud of their power and dignity. For some, it was a happy opportunity to govern the province and set their own agenda, manipulating their own citizens, particularly in rural areas such as Boumxieng Village. This region had flat lands between mountain ranges that were ideal for new development, including business towns, cities, and agriculture. For peasants, land was their life, but for the elites, land was a source of wealth and power. They bought land from the villagers at low, extortive prices to resell later to developers at multiples of what they paid. Those who refused to sell at the offered price were threatened by local authorities, often police officers.

The well-known organized crime boss in the region, General Mous, had learned from his father, General Sueke, how to make money on the side while holding a government position. After his father's death in 1991, Mous worked his way up from captain, and after upgrading his army skills in North Vietnam in 2001, was appointed general and posted in the Luang Prabang province. Like father like son, Mous had used his high position in the government and his skill at making money to run an underground gang, selling illegal lumber, drugs, and running prostitution. But it was only when he got into the land development game that he made his true fortune. Now Touy, his son was running the racket for him.

IT WAS on a Saturday morning that they rode to the city on her motorcycle for the first time. The memory of that day would stay with Sithana the rest of his life. Viengvilay had dressed like a westerner: blue jeans and a red top. They had stopped at a food stand along the river bank. Viengvilay was crying, telling him about her engagement to a man she didn't love as Sithana held her hand.

"I'm very happy to see you, Sith. I had a nightmare that I would never see you again... I'm glad you came back, even if it is in the worst circumstances...."

They watched the tourist boats pass each other on the river below as Viengvilay told her story.

Viengvilay had just graduated from Luang Prabang University with a degree in education in the winter of 2007. A year after submitting an application, she was granted her dream job of teaching back in her home village—the village she and Sithana had grown up in. One day, a man in his late twenties—Touy in a civil servant's uniform—visited her house to offer her father a job. Viengvilay was already living back home with her parents and teaching at the village elementary school by then.

"The following week, he came to my house again, but this time he only talked to my parents. He told my father that he had just purchased land up the river and offered my father the position of supervisor. The job involved supervising workers in the field and looking for new land for him to purchase, and reporting back to him in Townmu District, where his office was located. My father was proud to have the job offer and was excited to be paid three hundred a month... six times what he had been making before... fifty per month," she said, forcing a smile. "After taking the job, my father was able to buy land of his own and save for my future education. He even built a new house in the village," she said.

Sithana looked over the river and said, "That's a good thing, isn't it?"

"It was... But soon Touy was at my house a lot. One day, shortly after, he asked to take me to the city. I was very nervous, but my father told me that he worked for Touy and assured me that there was no harm in going with him. My father said I should get to know him better." Viengvilay fought back her tears. "We went driving along the Namkan river, a popular spot for young people and tourists to hang out. He stopped at a fancy hotel and told me that his father owned it, and that many of the guest houses on the same street also belonged to his family. He bragged about how he would eventually inherit all of these properties and how he was lucky to be the only son of an army general. I felt shy and his behavior and comments made me uncomfortable, but I kept my head down and didn't say much. I started to wonder if he had any destination in mind for the evening..." She looked at Sithana in the eyes. "Tell me if you don't want me to continue. I think it's important for you to know everything about my experience."

"Do continue," Sithana replied. "To be perfectly honest, I'm a little jealous that he was able to take you to all those luxurious places."

Viengvilay shook her head. "That means nothing to me... *He* means nothing to me."

Sithana couldn't hide his happiness at hearing this.

"When we got to the bridge, he asked if I was hungry. I said no, but we drove back to a well-known restaurant near the Mekong river anyway. He continued to brag about how many buildings in the area belonged to his father, including three brothels that he said were the source of most of their daily cash. After we finished eating, he drove me to one of the brothels. I saw young women with older men and saw young student girls serving alcohol to foreign tourists. At that point, I asked him to take me home. He nodded and agreed. We stopped at a drugstore nearby and he told me to wait in the car. He returned a few minutes later with a piece of gum and we both chewed it as he drove me home. The road was dusty and dark. The only vehicle on the road that evening was his black Land Rover. About eight or ten kilometers outside of town, there was a dense forest with a small path running under the tall trees. Beyond that was a rice field, large, but quiet and dark. He drove into it and stopped the SUV. 'Why did you stop here?' I asked. He didn't answer. He got out of his seat, walked past the front of the vehicle, and opened the door on my side…He pulled my legs out and pushed my head down against the passenger seat. I tried to push him off me, but couldn't…He lifted my skirt, high up until it covered my head. He penetrated me… When he finished, he pulled my skirt back down… he got back in his seat, started the car and drove off as if nothing had happened. I was crying and bleeding… He drops me off and says, 'I am sorry, I can't help myself, you are so beautiful.' I was speechless. I knew it then that he had planned this…"

Sithana dragged his chair closer to hers and leaned in. Their foreheads touched as Viengvilay again fought back the tears.

"I am so sorry this happened to you," Sithana told her. "It makes me very angry."

"It happened on Friday night. On Saturday, I went to your house to see your parents and Dara was there. She had no idea what had happened to me, and was full of joy at seeing me. She was such an innocent kid. I sat behind her and brushed her hair. Your father looked at me and I could tell he knew something was wrong. That's when he told me you were moving from Australia to Canada and had lost contact with them. He said they hadn't heard from you in a long time. Dara told me she hadn't received any letters from you in almost six months and she was afraid she would never see you again. She said she wanted to leave the village and go somewhere far away where no one could find her, just like you, her brother."

Viengvilay could no longer hold the tears back. She was crying hard. "You're lucky to have gotten out. You never saw or experienced the abuse of these tyrants; but I am trapped in the tyrant's circle and see no way out."

"You are helping me," Sithana ventured, "and so I will help you."

Viengvilay ignored his offer and went on: "The following Monday morning, Touy and one of his associates came to the school, but found out I wasn't there that day teaching. Someone must have told him that I wasn't feeling well. He rushed to my house immediately. I was lying on the bed with my right arm on my forehead, still crying when he arrived. He came in, seeing me in that condition, asked his men to wait outside. He sat next to me and told me he was sorry. Then he put his hand on my head to caress it. It was more than I could bear. I pushed his hand away. It made him angry. 'I am here today to propose an engagement,' he told me. I was shaking my head. 'If you had any respect for me,' he then said, 'I wouldn't have needed to force myself on you. And here you are disrespecting me again. It's all your fault. You have no one to blame but yourself,' he told me. The anger rose inside of me. It was so powerful and I wanted to kill him right where he was sitting with whatever weapon I could find. 'I will speak to your father,' he said; and I knew I was done for. I can't go against my father's wishes...I prayed that I would never see him again. But soon, I received an envelope addressed to me at the house. I opened it and before reading the note, I saw a thick gold necklace. In Laos, this value of that necklace could be used to build a two-bedroom wooden house. I felt horrible—conflicted and disgusted all at once. 'I am the only man in this world that can have you, no one can take you away from me,' he wrote in his note. I gave the necklace to my father along with the note, hoping he would return it out of pride, but he didn't... The note went on to describe his plan and date for the engagement. He wanted to celebrate the engagement and was hosting a party. His parents and extended family would attend. A month later, there was a large crowd, more than a couple hundred people gathered for our engagement. The thought that this was a farce, a hellish irony, hung over me. Everyone seemed happy—my father especially. No one bothered about my happiness or could even see how miserable I was… Everyone except your parents. I began to spend more and more time with them."

Viengvilay leaned back and seemed to be lost in thought as she recalled those days. She remembered them vividly, like a movie reel. She remembered the feeling of dread that had filled her and the impending sense of doom that hung over her. Then when Sithana showed up, asking for her help with his family's funeral, she knew that her fears were well-founded. But despite the risks, she knew that she had to help him. She couldn't turn her back on him, or on the memory of her childhood friend Dara. And so she agreed to do whatever she could to help Sithana, even if it meant putting her own life in danger.

IV

4 months ago. The night before the fire.

THE evening before she and her family were killed, Dara had told Viengvilay that one of her cows had just given birth. Viengvilay asked to see the young calf, but Dara told her to wait until the next morning. "It's getting too dark now," she said. After Dara left, Viengvilay's father told her not to spend too much time with Dara, saying that she was now a big girl and no longer needed a babysitter. When Viengvilay sat down, both her parents looked at her before looking at each other and sucking their lips in between their teeth. Viengvilay couldn't understand if they were trying to tell her to save time for other things or if they just didn't like the idea of her liking Dara's family so much and visiting them often. She kept silent and went to bed with many the conversation turning in her head.

MEANWHILE, at that very same time, Khamhuck and his two friends were crossing the Mekong that night. Chur drove the grey Mazda pickup onto the ferry. Soud and Khamhuck were out on the deck for a smoke. Both tossed their half-burning cigarettes away and went back to their seats. "We have to get drunk," said Soud. All three nodded in agreement. Chur pushed on the gas coming off the ferry to have more power for going up the hill. Soud and Khamhuck were laughing hysterically, even though nothing was particularly funny. Each of them had taken two *yama* pills—a drug made specifically for horses, but creating euphoria and a sense of invincibility in humans who ingested it.

Chur had parked the pick-up at the beer stand beside the road moments later and ordered a case of twelve bottles of lager. He handed each one of them a bottle and they started drinking next to the stand.

"We will be back in a couple of hours, and we'll drink again!" Khamhuck said to the woman. The men laughed.

The woman was indifferent. "Okay," she said.

"Before the ferry closes," he added. "In a couple of hours, like I said. Will you still be open?"

"No problem," she told him, without looking up. "If closed, then knock on the door," she said.

"Perfect!" Khamhuck exclaimed. "We won't know how late we'll be. We are off to a friend's birthday party," Khamhuck said turning to the other two. They all broke out laughing and the old woman smiled crookedly as if hiding her disgust. Then Khamhuck took six pills out from his shirt pocket and gave two to each of his friends. He opened his mouth, dropped the pills in, and finished the bottle of beer. "That'll do," he mumbled. The woman watched them suspiciously as they walked off to the truck and sped off towards the village.

IN her dreams that night, Viengvilay saw the two coconut trees in her backyard fall to the ground. She went to look for the cause of their fall, but saw nothing. When she turned back to the house and looked again, both of the trees had disappeared. She called for her father to come see, but he looked at her, turned his back on her, and walked away. The coconuts had been there before she was born. She used to run around them as a kid. To lose them was significant. They were symbols of her childhood. She went into the house, but neither her mother nor father was there. She called for them, and the next thing she awoke and realized it had all been a dream. She went back to sleep, but couldn't quell a nagging sense of dread.

The next morning, Viengvilay went to visit Dara and see the newborn calf. As she walked towards Dara's house, she couldn't shake the feeling that her dream from the night before was a warning of some sort. When she arrived, Dara was outside feeding the calf.

"Look, Viengvilay," she said, smiling. "He's so cute!"

Viengvilay smiled back and tried to push her negative thoughts aside. She spent the morning with Dara and her family, helping with chores and trying to enjoy the moment. But as the day went on, she couldn't shake the feeling again that something was about to go terribly wrong. That afternoon, Viengvilay returned home and found her parents waiting for her.

"We need to talk to you," her mother said, a worried look on her face. "It's about Touy."

Viengvilay's heart sank. She had been dreading this conversation for a long time. "What about him?" she asked, trying to keep her voice steady.

"He wants to marry you," her father said. "And we think it's a good idea."

Viengvilay couldn't believe what she was hearing. "But I don't love him," she protested. "I don't want to marry him."

Her parents looked at each other, then back at Viengvilay. "We understand that," her mother said. "But he's a good man, and he can provide for you. And it would be good for our family to have a connection with his."

Viengvilay couldn't believe what she was hearing. She knew that her parents meant well, but she couldn't imagine spending the rest of her life with someone she didn't love. And she was worried about the danger that being connected to Touy's family might bring. But she knew that arguing with her parents would be futile. So she reluctantly agreed to meet with Touy and discuss the matter further. As the days went on, Viengvilay couldn't suppress the intuition that something terrible was about to happen.

THAT NIGHT, like every night in the village, was quiet, but before closing her eyes, Viengvilay heard the sound of a car passing on the road above her house. She thought the speed was over the limit, very fast, as if someone was chasing someone else, but she had no reason to go out and take a look. The Boumxieng village was located on a flat piece of land alongside the Xieng River. The road was built on higher ground, starting at the Mekong shore in Jomphet District and running about thirteen kilometers to the village. Inside the village, there were many passages that small vehicles could access, but no permanent road. The three men parked their pickup truck on the road. Khamhuck turned on the compartment light, took out a piece of paper that someone inside had drawn for them, indicating each room in the house, and noting what they should do first. Then they took their two military canvas bags from the cargo bed and walked directly to the house. Chur took out a small crowbar from his bag and used it to pry open the wooden door as Soud held the flashlight for him. Then all three men went inside at the same time. Once in the main hall, Khamhuck, pointed to

Soud to go to the master bedroom where the parents were asleep. Chur walked straight to the smaller room which was Dara's bedroom, and Khamhuck went to the right, to Lium's room. Chur saw Dara sleeping. It was a hot night and she had kicked the sheets off her body and way lying there exposed, half-naked. Chur shone the flashlight on her up and down, avoiding her face. He tip-toed to the bed and knelt down beside her. Then he aggressively put his hand on her mouth, pushing down very hard. He pulled down his own pants and rolled on top of her and began raping her. As she struggled to breathe and fought to get up, he used his left hand to cover her mouth and his right hand to pull out a knife from his right hip. He pushed the knife into her throat until he was sure she had stopped breathing. In the room next to them, was Khamhuck, strangling Lium with a nylon line. Some of the commotion must have woken Mrs. Pathavong. She stirred in her bed and called out for Dara. "What is the noise there?" she asked. Panicking, Soud shot both husband and wife in the head. Khamhuck came out of the bedroom, calling for his men. There was no sense in hiding anymore. They poured gasoline over the beds and the bodies and then whatever was left over the rest of the house. Minutes later they were downstairs kneeling over the bag they had left at the entrance. Khamhuck opened the bag and Chur and Soud took out the grenades. They pulled the pins, threw the grenades into the house through the front door and took off running. The explosion was so powerful that it destroyed everything and burned the entire house to the ground.

Khamhuck never looked back but rushed to the pickup truck, got in, and told his men to drive off. They sped past the beer stand, not stopping as they had said they would. Even so, they had missed the last ferry by the time they arrived. Khamhuck decided they would hide themselves and the truck in the bush until morning. They turned the headlights off and veered off the road for awhile and then parked.

Meanwhile, back at the village, the explosion had woken everyone. Now the fire was lighing up the night sky. Viengvilay had run out of the house in her pajamas to join all the other villagers running toward the scene. As she got closer, she began to fear it had been Dara's house. The area was so crowded with people and everyone trying to abate the flames, running back and forth with anything they could use to carry water. It took Viengvilay awhile before the realization sunk in. She collapsed near a tree beside the house, watching the flames shoot up high like the tip of a spear. Tears flowed down her face. "Sky... Sky... My dear Dara! Come Dara, come. I am here!" she repeated over and over again.

THERE was a sliver of sun beginning to rise above the water in the sky when the boat touched land. Khamhuck was impatient and nervous. As soon as the line of cars began moving forward, he over accelerated and almost hit the bumper of the car ahead of them. The ferryman was watching from his booth and made a note of the license plate numbers.

He had taken notice of them upon entry. They were the first in line and looked to him like they had been waiting there all night. After they drove the truck onto the ferry, he approached them. He stood at the passenger side to collect the fare. One of the men rolled down the window and handed him the money. He noticed two other men. He stepped back to look at the truck's cargo bed. The man who handed him the money had panicked. He got out of the truck. "You need something else?" he had asked him.

He had made him nervous. There was a look in his eyes as he had gotten out of the truck. "Your right wheels are parked too close to the edge," the ferry man had told him. "Be careful when you pull out and off the boat."

"Will do," Khamhuck had answered, and sat back in his seat.

The ferry man returned to his booth but not before he noticed that one of the men in the truck was bleeding from a cut on his cheek. He was covered in scratches and was missing a sleeve as though it had been torn off.

Then later that morning, on his second round trip, the ferryman who always kept the radio on caught the broadcaster announcing an explosion in the area resulting in a number of casualties. "Last night after midnight, police station six received a call from the mayor of Boumxieng reporting that there was a loud explosion, and the house was completely burned with four dead in the family," the broadcaster informed. Details of the radio announcement continued for the next three minutes, but no police interviews were aired.

KHAMHUCK and his men returned to the hotel they had rented, cleaned up and then went to meet Touy at one of the many bars he owned.

"Here is your share," said Touy. He handed a brown envelope to each of them. They all opened it at the same time and started counting the cash.

"As I promised, gentlemen," Touy said. "Eight thousand US for the job."

Each man received $2,666. After counting, Chur and Soud each gave Khamhuck an extra hundred dollars— his cut as their leader. They would not have had the job without him. It was seen as paying respect and dues.

"Well done, gentlemen," Touy said. He raised a bottle in a toast and smiled. "I am thanking you and will be in touch."

Everyone raised their bottles though their faces showed no happiness or joy. They left, one after another, in Touy's footsteps. Khamhuck and Chur looked at each other and shrugged their shoulders. There was no use in sticking around and they decided to leave as well.

Then on the road headed north from the bar and the Mekong River, Chur broke the silence that had filled the truck since they got in.

"I raped her," Chur said, through a thick cloud of smoke.

Khamhuck wasn't sure he had heard correctly. "You what?" he growled.

"I said I raped the girl," Chur repeated.

"You fucking did what?!" Khamhuck screamed. "How can a fucking limp dick piece of shit like you even get it up?" He turned around in his head and hit him hard, until he was bleeding. Soud pulled off to the side of the road. Khamhuck dragged Chur out of the car and to the edge of the cliff. Chur was begging for his life. Soud feared the worst and tried to hold Khamhuck back.

"We shouldn't have taken those yama pills in the first place," he said.

Khamhuck looked Soud in the eyes and calmed down after realizing he was partly to blame—the pills had made Chur's mind regress from human to animal. Khamhuck kicked Chur once again for good measure, but let him go. He leaned down and spoke in his Chur's ear. "If you ever do anything like that again, I'll cut your balls off and let you hobble around for some years before I finish you off." He shoved Soud on his way back to the truck. "Everybody in," he ordered.

THE sky was covered with dark clouds, but was turning red toward the west. It was almost five PM and the sun was leaving a red trail before it set. Thong, the ferry man, was on his way home from work. Meanwhile a thought had been repeatedly turning over in his mind that the three men he had seen in the pickup might have had something to do with the explosion.

His wife had already heard about the explosion and the fire by the time he got home from work that evening. "Have you heard?" she asked excitedly, coming to the door the minute she heard him.

Thong let her tell him all about it. It was only when she seemed done and spent from the excitement of the news that he spoke.

"I know... These men in a truck came on the ferry, today," he told his wife. "I had the impression they had something to do with the explosion."

"You mean you *know* they did," his wife said. "I'm

always telling you to listen to your instincts," she reminded him. "Stop being such a coward! We have to keep our family safe... We know nothing. Remember what I tell you!"

Thong bit his lip, nodding. Everyone knew what was going on, but everyone was afraid to speak out. The whole village went on living their lives as if they were buffalo in a herd, grazing like nothing had happened... All except Thong.

THE NEXT morning, police came and asked Thong if any suspicious men had boarded the ferry the night before. "Did you see any suspicious men or women on your boat yesterday?"

Thong fretted, looked around for his wife, who was outside tending to the livestock, and finally answered. "I may have."

"I'll tell you what," the police officer said. "You have a choice. First, you can tell the federal police what you have seen and never see your family again; or you can keep your mouth shut, take this money...and who knows, the boss might like you," he said flashing Thong two hundred US dollars. "Hey you can buy yourself a new boat. What do you say?" he asked, tapping Thong on the cheek. It was half a slap. Thong nodded and took the money. He glimpsed at the police car and saw three boys sitting, handcuffed in the back seat. His heart sank, but he wanted to live. He learned later from the news that one of the boys was Dara's boyfriend. When he told his wife, she thought he had made a wise decision. There was no right or wrong, good or bad in her mind. It was a matter of life and death. Thong's decision that day helped his family prolong their lives. They might soon be killed also, but at least not today.

VIENGVILAY was beside herself all morning that day. She woke up to see most of her neighbors marching to the scene of the crime. She rushed to the house and saw Bouy crying hard, leaning on the fence beside the burned house. Ken was holding her calmly.

"What happened, Ken? Do you know the cause yet?" Viengvilay asked.

"Some crazy, stupid kids tossed a grenade and killed them," Ken said.

"Kids?" Viengvilay repeated incredulously. She walked around, waiting for the fire truck and police to come so she could learn more about the incident.

Ken saw her loitering about and finally approached her. "I would go to work and leave this to the police if I were you. There is nothing you and I can do. I know it is hard...for us too. It's our family," Ken told her.

V

SITHANA felt safe and comfortable locked away alone in his hotel room. He tried not to dwell too much on his dead family, but instead on Viengvilay, who had come to visit.

"I forgot to tell you: the boy is dead," she was saying.

"No, you already told me," he reminded her.

"Tieng, Dara's friend?" she asked.

"Yes," he said. "You told me he was dead, but you did not tell me how or why."

"Right, I didn't," she said. "You need to be careful and not go near the shore alone."

Sithana fell silent, listening to what she had to say. He wasn't sure he wanted to hear all the details of how the boy was killed. He was angry not only about the boy's death, but also about how his own plan to bring the family home from the woods to recover their remains was being thwarted. Now he thought the plan might have to be postponed or even canceled, though he would try not to let that happen. He knew Touy would do anything to stop him from transferring the remains and reclaiming Viengvilay—and it was all out of pettiness and jealousy:

because he knew she would never love him. Sithana now realized that Touy would never allow his family to take the remains elsewhere. Viengvilay had already confessed that Touy had ordered his men to watch her and to stop her from going anywhere. Apparently, Touy flew into a fit of rage when he learned that Viengvilay had taken a week off to "help a friend prepare for a funeral".

Indeed, after Sithana's arrival in the village, Viengvilay had spent most of her weekends and free time with Sithana, avoiding Touy as much as she could. The villagers were starting to talk. Sithana felt that what he had come for, his family, was no longer a priority now, but Viengvilay's safety was becoming the more pressing concern.

Consequently, it was not only her safety at stake, but his as well. She reminded him, the simplest solution to everyone's problems here would be for him to "disappear" and go the way of the rest of his family. These men would stop at nothing she explained. She was telling him how the police had beaten Tieng for days until they forced a confession out him and his friends. He was innocent of course. Everyone knew that. He was in love with Dara and would never do anything to harm her. He would always go about the village bragging that she loved him too, and that he would soon get a job in the city and buy the biggest house and take Dara there... But the police told another story. They made him sign a statement confessing that he had killed them out of jealousy, because Sithana's father had refused Tieng's courtship of his daughter.

Of course, he too, was killed before he could defend his innocence.

✳✳✳

IT was about approximately four months ago. Touy was reading the news, nodding and smiling, believing the whole town to be on his side. The newspaper reporter even questioned the ferryman who of course said that he was always too busy to notice any of the passengers.

Touy was confident his men had left no trace. They were organized and even in the worst case, they had the money to buy people's silence. So once Touy had received the official report of the signed confessions and that the police had caught the killers, Touy told the chief of Station Six to do whatever was necessary to end the case for good. That's when Tieng's death sentence was signed. Then one morning, after he had finished the breakfast that was brought to him, Tieng was sitting on the tiny bed looking toward the gate, hoping his mother would come to take him home, when the police appeared at the outer gate. Minutes later he saw one of them walk by his cell and the second one who looked meaner, stopped and looked him straight in the eye through the bars.

"Come closer, boy," he commanded.

Tieng moved closer as ordered.

"Closer," I said.

Tieng moved another step closer.

"Listen, my son," he said to Ting. "I have a boy the same age as you," he said. "I have wanted to save your life from the very beginning, ever since I brought you here... but you didn't listen to me."

Tieng was confused, but he wouldn't give the policeman the satisfaction. He looked straight ahead and didn't say a word.

"Today will be your last day here," he went on telling him. "It saddens me."

Tieng could see that the policeman was indeed affected. It was almost more than Tieng could bear. He made a move to step away.

"I told you to stand there," he shouted, angry now. "And don't move!"

Tieng faced forward again. The policeman took his keys out, opened the cell door and stepped inside the cage. There was a fierce, pitiless look on his face.

"We're going to play a game," he said. "You see these keys here? You can have them and your freedom if you can get them off me."

His partner waiting in the hall, snickered. Moments

later a shot rang out and Tieng was falling backwards bleeding from his forehead. Later the evening news reported that Tieng, the murder suspect, had attacked a policeman attempting to obtain a police key and then a gun to escape. The police officer in question had been forced to shoot him in self-defence.

※※※

VIENGVILAY didn't want to risk being seen with Sithana. She left the hotel room at the break of dawn, leaving a note on the lamp table that said, "Please do not return to the village. It is not safe."

Sithana hesitated, but then decided it best to find another hotel. He left the room first thing after breakfast and took a cab to another hotel that was not in the center of town. At the moment, he was more worried about Viengvilay than his own safety. He believed that her life and family were in danger, and all because of him.

Now alone again, in a room on the third floor, Sithana was growing restless. He couldn't return to the village and it was no longer safe to go out and play the tourist. With nothing to do but fret and worry about Viengvilay's safety and justice for his family's murders, Sithana paced the whole day, walking about his room until it tired him out. He pulled a chair to the window and sat looking out over the narrow walkway behind the hotel. He watched the women walking past beneath his window carrying vegetables, live chickens and ducks to sell at the nearby market. He was almost falling asleep when he heard a knock at the door.

Sithana rose and opened the door to see a short, corpulent man in the eggshell color of a civil servant's uniform.

"Mr. Sithana Pathavong?" he asked. "I found your name on the hotel registration."

"Yes, it's me. What can I do for you?"

"If you do not mind, Mr. Pathavong, I'd like to talk to you in private," the man said. "May I step inside for a moment?"

Sithana noticed that he may have been stout, but he was a fast talker and a jittery sort of man. Sithana stepped back to let the man in. He sat down on the couch and made himself comfortable without hesitation, letting out a deep breath and spreading his legs open.

"Sit down, Sithana," he said. "Take a deep breath… You may not know me, but I know who you are through Miss Viengvilay. She has spoken of you often since you arrived… No I am not from the village, but I have lived in the same district. I have been teaching in the same school as Viengvilay for three years now, and I love the place…"

Sithana looked at him intently, waiting for what it was he wanted to say.

"My point is…" he said, smiling crookedly. "I mean… You should know that the school is funded mostly by private donors, mainly Viengvilay's fiancé's real estate company. I'm not sure the school or many other schools in the area, would survive without their generosity."

Sithana was silent. He knew it would be wiser in this situation to hold his tongue; but he couldn't help himself.

"You say you are Viengvilay's friend… Well, then… Suppose you are engaged to a rich man you do not love, but your parents tell you to marry him, and you have very little time left before your wedding date… and he owns the school you work in and runs the town you live in… and then… and then… suddenly you meet a man and fall madly in love with him, what would you do?" he asked.

The man looked uncomfortable for the first time since he arrived, Sithana thought and smiled. The man shifted in his seat.

"What I am saying is that it would be safer for all of us if you did not stay here too long," he explained. He got up to leave. "I suggest you leave town as soon as possible. You can tell me what you would like done regarding your family's remains and I promise I will get it done. Free of charge."

The man looked Sithana in the eyes. "His eyeball is as big as goat's eye," Sithana thought and fell silent.

"You look pale," the man said. "We can talk another time. My name is Chanta, by the way... You can trust me. I'll see to it that everything gets done the way you want it." He began walking towards the door. "You are having a negative impact on our community with your presence. Remember, you're a foreigner now, brother. Please understand..." And then turning around at the door, like an afterthought, he said, "I'll let Viengvilay know where you are and give her your regards."

Sithana sat back down on the couch, sweating and trembling. All he could think about now were the thinly veiled threats this man, Chanta, had made. It's like he had been living a movie until now—even the sorrow and tragedy of his family's murder hadn't hit him fully. He had been playing the part in some kind of romantic thriller. But it was hitting home now: the threats were very real and he was realizing that there was no place for him to hide. *I found your name in a hotel book*, the man had said. He meant the guest list, of course. He was laying it out for Sithana and that's when Sithana finally understood. *You can change hotels all you want.* There wasn't even much of a need to track his movements, though everyone would take note of the foreigner—especially if he was going about town poking his nose in police matters. But if you wanted to find someone... if *Touy* wanted to find someone, is what he thought... there were only a handful of hotels. You could check each one until you found your man. How much easier wouldn't it be, if you already owned those hotels and employed half the town?

Sithana was panicking. *Don't go to the village*, Viengvilay had advised him. How did that change anything? They had just showed him that if they wanted to find him, they would find him easily enough... and Viengvilay and his aunt and uncle would always be exposed. There was nothing he could do to protect any of them, except leave.

❋❋❋

CHANTA confronted Viengvilay at her work that very Monday. The school day had just ended and he walked in just as the last students were filing out.

"I went to see your foreigner friend Sunday morning," he said. "At the Phousy Hotel...That's where he's staying now. We spoke at length upon the matter of his family and the... unfortunate accident. I told him it was best for everyone if he left the country. He's a foreigner to us now. I think he agreed."

Viengvilay's jaw was hanging open. She was still at her

desk. She rose at once. "You did what? Why, why did you do that? How… Who told you to do that?"

"Listen, we all knew what you did was wrong. For all our sakes, including yours, he has to go. We care about you, sister."

"Don't call me sister again!" Viengvilay fumed, enraged. "I am not your sister! You are a pathetic lap dog. What I do is none of your business. Leave us alone!"

"All I'm trying to do is help you, and you know it."

"I don't need your help! You piece of cow shit! Get out!" she yelled, pointing at the door.

Viengvilay shut the door behind him, and turned, leaning against the wall, fighting back her tears. Then on her way out, standing by the exit doors was the principal. He had a worried look on his face. He had heard the commotion minutes ago, and had already heard all the village gossip.

"Just know that I, my family, and all the teachers and staff are here for you, but… Perhaps you should take some time off? For the sake of the children… I mean…"

Viengvilay turned to look him in the eyes, but the old man turned his face away.

❈❈❈

CHANTA meanwhile had gone to meet Touy at a restaurant in town as they agreed. He sat and waited for thirty minutes, considering whether to tell him about Viengvilay's reaction after he told her that Sithana should leave. However, he was not quite sure of himself. By the time Touy was walking through the doors, Chanta had changed his mind and decided not to mention Viengvilay, but only talk about Sithana.

"So, I confronted the man," Chanta told Touy. "He seems like a smart and nice guy."

"Really?" he said with disgust. "Did you make friends?" He spat on the floor. "I don't want to know what he's like. Just tell me what happened. Is he leaving?"

Chanta sipped his coffee nervously. "I think so."

"You *think so*?" Tuoy looked up at the sky in disbelief. He returned his gaze at Chanta, shaking his head and twisting his nose in anger.

Chanta was quick to explain himself. "His only concern is his family's remains. Once that's resolved, he will return home. It was never his intention to stay long in Laos. Even while talking to me, he used a mix of Lao and English. He barely speaks our language. He's a foreigner now. Viengvilay must pity him, that's must be the only reason she—"

"Don't talk about her," Tuoy warned him; but it had

mollified him. He appeared relieved and sat back in his chair more relaxed.

It was all jealousy Chanta thought; petty jealousy and nothing more. Now, he regretted having confronted Viengvilay and all that he had said to her. He considered her a sister, but was suddenly ashamed of seeing her again.

❋❋❋

VIENGVILAY'S father was waiting for her when she arrived home. He was irate. "People know that you go to the city to see him… You come back the next morning. I know what you are doing! It is shameful! It is an embarrassment to me and your mother! Is this how we raised you? You are engaged!"

Viengvilay was on the verge of tears. It was all too much to handle at the moment.

"It wasn't safe for him to stay at his aunt's… I wanted to make sure he was safe," she explained. Viengvilay looked at her mother who turned away.

"People talk…" she said in a defeated voice.

Viengvilay broke out in tears. She loved her family deeply. But she felt they were being selfish and dishonorable while she was following her heart. And yes! That's just how they raised her and she was proud of it. How could they have forgotten that and who they were! She was old enough to know the facts of life and understood that money was everyone's main concern. But was Touy's money and power, all it took for her family to give up on their principles? The whole town? With time she had learned with greater detail what it was exactly that her father was doing for Touy. It sickened her to know her father had been visiting all the farms in the neighbouring lands trying convince poor land owners to sell their properties for small cash payments. Everyone knew what the threat was if they refused. Everyone had heard what happened to families like Sithana's. Often times, they would poison that family's livestock before paying them a visit. Besides the obvious implication of 'you're next', it made it clear to the family that their farms would never again be allowed to be profitable… Everyone sold, sooner or later. That created another problem: Most of those families had worked that farmland for generations and knew nothing else. They were promised that they would be allowed to stay and work the lands and receive a salary on top of the sale. That never happened. Their lands became garbage dumping grounds overnight. Large transport trucks would come in and dump their loads of trash onto the fields. This created a health and rat hazard that acted as an added incentive for the neighbouring farms to sell and sell quickly. It was a perfect hell, she thought.

"Do you know that most of the hotels and guesthouses in Luang Prabang are owned by Touy's family?" her father remind her.

Viengvilay still in tears, shrugged to show her indifference.

"Those people working in the hotels are all friends of the family if they're not direct relatives."

"He says they own them, but I'm not sure. He brags a lot..." Viengvilay retorted.

"Well, they do! They own most of them, if not all of them."

"I don't care about that father... I don't want to know." Viengvilay pleaded.

"But you need to know because soon you will become a member of his family and legally be an owner. You understand?"

"Dad, please stop. I'm embarrassed by what you're saying," Viengvilay begged.

Her father grabbed her arm and turned her towards him. "Look at me, young lady. You have a long life ahead of you and I'm concerned. I don't want you to go through what your mother and I went through. We struggled to survive and support your education. You have a great opportunity, don't let it slip away. We've been doing everything for your own good." He let out a deep breath and appeared to calm down. He looked at his wife and then said, "Your mother and I wish you to stop seeing that young man, Sithana. We have decided: You will not see him again."

Viengvilay pulled away. "Mother, Father! Sithana came back here for one thing only—his sacred duty to relocate his family's remains to holy ground. We would all want and do the same if it happened to us. His sister was my dear friend and his parents have always been kind to me. Now his aunt and uncle don't know how to read and he can't help them... He was forced to leave his home and our country to flee persecution... and how they're doing it again! I am just trying to help him bury his family's remains. Nothing else! I haven't done anything wrong!"

"We just want you to be careful," her mother said, from her seat at the table.

"Of course, Mama!" she comforted, but she knew, she was already too far out in uncharted territory to ever find her way back.

VI

KHAMHUCK had stopped by the bamboo shack where his sister and her family lived and gave her money equivalent to $90, which was two months' salary for a transport truck driver in the country.

"What did you do to get this money?" his sister asked.

"I sell medicines," Khamhuck replied.

"What kinds?" she asked.

"All kinds that people need," he replied.

"I need headache pills. Can you give me some?" she asked.

"I'll bring you some tomorrow," Khamhuck said without thinking.

Over a year had passed since Khamhuck's brother-in-law was killed in an accident. Toulee, the husband of Khamhuck's only sister, had worked for an illegal Chinese logging company for a couple of years until his death over a year ago. While cutting down a large tree, he heard the crack, pulled out his chainsaw and ran, trying to get far enough away to avoid being hit by the trunk. However, his forehead hit a small tree, and as he turned back towards the trunk, he was hit in the head and killed instantly. He left his wife and two children with no income.

Khamhuck got into his pickup truck and drove away, leaving a cloud of dust behind him as his two nephews ran after him to the main road. His sister and the two boys had no idea what Khamhuck was up to, but they were grateful for his generosity, as it helped them to have food and shelter. They saw him as a hero.

Chur and Soud were waiting for Khamhuck next to a bus station in the Naphtha district. Chur approached Khamhuck as he was getting out of his truck.

"They're waiting in the hotel room," Chur told him.

"I know," Khamhuck replied. "They texted me earlier."

"You didn't tell us?" Soud remarked. Soud and Chur looked at each other.

"I've been busy," Khamhuck said. "Anyway, what does it matter? You idiots had something better to do?" Khamhuck spat on the ground. "Let's go…"

The trio arrived at a white building with wooden frames that looked like a cheap hotel for young backpackers.

"What room are they in?" Khamhuck asked.

"Four," Soud said.

They walked in. The young man at the front counter recognized them, rose from his seat and went into the back office.

Khamhuck knocked at the door and Yeen, a small woman in her thirties with long black hair and dark eyes opened the door.

"Come in," she said, smiling. "My friends are here."

They were led to a large room with twin beds, blue cushions, and a carpeted floor. Within were two other Chinese women who stood up to greet them.

"Let's have a drink, yes?" Yeen said. She poured out shots of something that looked like tea. They all sipped it and soon found their mood changing. Khamhuck too, was beginning to relax. He liked Yeen. He thought of most women as dead, wilted flowers... but Yeen was different. She was a powerful boss and connected. Under the effects of that concoction, he was wondering what it would be like to make love to a woman like Yeen... to visit China... to be a boss himself.

Yeen noticed the men and her girls were starting to have a little too much fun. She clapped her hands and the girls rose to their feet and went into the adjacent room. Yeen opened a drawer and reached inside it. Khamhuck saw a handgun and brown paper bag. Yeen went for the paper bag and handed it to Khamhuck.

"There's six thousand dollars there," she said.

The girls came out with two cardboard boxes handing one each to Chur and Soud.

Yeen then gave Khamhuck a slip of paper. The address of a wildlife restaurant about thirty kilometers north of Luang Prabang was written on it.

"The drop-off has changed. This is not the same address," he said, stuffing the paper in his pocket.

"No, it's not," Yeen replied. "It's a better location. Quiet... country road... Less risk."

Yeen made a motion with her hand toward the door. It was the sign for them to leave.

"I don't think I need to remind you boys what will happen to you if those boxes aren't delivered."

Khamhuck nodded and Yeen closed the door behind them.

He had always been a man on the run. He started smoking opium as a teenager. When he had no money to buy the drug, he began stealing rice from poor farmers, then their pigs and chickens selling it all at half price in the market. When the villagers caught him, his mother sold their only buffalo to pay for his crime and told him to leave home and never return.

So, yeah... with the years, Khamhuck had learned a couple of tricks on how to live on the run. He opened the back door of the truck and reached beneath the back seat for a hidden button. Finding it, he pressed it and the back seats popped open to reveal a hidden compartment. Chur and Soud each placed their boxes inside before Khamhuck snapped the seats back in place. He turned around before getting into driver's seat to see Yeen watching from the room window. He got in and drove off.

It was all harmless at first. Stealing from neighbours to buy drugs was the worst he had done. There had been no violence… Then he met Chur and Soud and the gang was formed. Setting the Pathavong's family home on fire and murdering everyone within wasn't the first horrific crime he was now responsible for. He wondered sometimes how he had grown so numb.

※※※※

OUDOMWAY and Luang Prabang are approximately forty kilometers apart. As they drove towards the southeast the sun shone on the windshield, almost blinding Soud who was driving too fast anyway. Then further on, a police car passed them in the opposite direction. Chur noticed the policemen trying to take stock of them. When he looked through the back window, he saw that the police had turned around to pursue them.

"Shit!" he exclaimed. "You're driving fast… The police are turning around."

"I'm driving too fast?" Soud wondered out loud. "Do you see any speed limit signs on this shit road?"

"Drive faster, you fucking turtle," Khamhuck told Soud, but the police car was already coming up behind them.

The police turned on its roof beacon lights. They heard "Pull over!" come from the megaphone.

Soud slowly pulled off the road. Khamhuck got ready. He took out a pistol from the compartment and hid it beneath his shirt, as he leaned into the side view mirror just in time to see the driver's side door on the police car open.

A policeman stepped out. Soud peered at the rear view mirror. "He's not alone," he said.

Khamhuck leaned in again toward the side mirror to get a better view. "Keep cool, boys," he said. "Let me handle this."

The officer had reached their car by then. He walked up to the driver's window where Soud was sitting, like a deer caught in headlights, looking dead in his seat, staring blankly ahead of him.

"In a hurry aren't you?" the policeman told Soud. "Where you going in such a hurry?"

"We are picking up a friend at a bus station in Oudomway," Khamhuck broke in.

The policeman looked at Khamhuck. "I wasn't talking to you," he said.

"That's a long trip to pick up a friend..." he said, turning to Soud again. "Why didn't he take the bus closer to you, huh?"

Soud shrugged. The policeman then looked in the

back seat at Chur who was trying to look calm and disinterested.

"And another long trip back... With two in the back seat. Not very comfortable..." the policeman said. "You bringing gifts for your friend, eh? What are you carrying?"

The police officer stepped back from their car and rested his hand on the gun in his hip holster. "Why don't you all step out of the truck for a minute..." he said.

All three stepped out of the truck as instructed. The police officer began inspecting the truck's interior as his partner got out of the police car to watch Khamhuck and his men.

"What's this on the back seat?" he asked.

"Just blankets, officer," Khamhuck answered.

"Blankets, eh?" He looked at his partner with amusement. "What are the blankets for? You cold in this heat?"

Khamhuck sneered. "It's none of your business."

"None of my business?" he repeated looking at his partner in amusement again. "Did you hear that? None of my business... Well, in our *business*, we often come across people who think they are being clever by hiding things under the seat," he added, laughing.

The policeman went for the blankets and Khamhuck knew the jig was up. He grabbed the officer who was bent over with his head in the car, and threw him back into the ditch behind them. The second officer went for his gun. Before he could reach it, Khamhuck pulled his own gun and shot him in the chest three times. They watched him fall to the floor and then roll off into the ditch and then down the hill to the creek. The first police officer who had been hurt when he was thrown, was now limping his way back to his car. Khamhuck walked up to him calmly and shot him from behind. He fell face down.

"I told you, it's none of your business," Khamhuck said and then shot him again for good measure.

Fairly sure the two policemen were dead, Khamhuck and his men got back in their truck and sped off. Behind them, the second officer was trying to crawl his way back up the hill to his partner who lay dead next to their police cruiser.

⁂

THE Wildlife Restaurant was on the outskirts of a national park. Built like a traditional hut from the outside, it had fortified cement interiors that belied its modern construction. It would not have been an easy feat to get all those imported materials into that remote area surrounded as it was by jungle and bamboo.

Soud backed the truck up to the back door as instructed.

They all got out and entered the restaurant through the delivery doors, Khamhuck walking ahead and Soud and Chur carrying the boxes behind him. They made their way through the storeroom, then the kitchen toward the back office.

Mr. Chanepeng had been waiting for them. As soon as they entered, he stood up, greeting them with a big smile and shaking hands with Khamhuck.

Soud and Chur rested their boxes on the desk.

"Thank you, gentlemen," Chanepeng said. "Please stay for lunch. The food here is all fresh game. We have some delicacies, you should try."

Chur and Soud looked excited at the prospect.

"I have heard," said Khamhuck. "Perhaps some other time… We're in a hurry today."

"What a shame!" Chanepeng said. "You've come all this way… Well, next time."

GETTING back into the truck, the men were just in time to catch a glimpse of two police cruisers speeding down the road they had just arrived from. They pulled off slowly. The usual road home took them back through the scene of the crime and a possible road block which was best to avoid.

"Let's take the road through town," Khamhuck said.

"Take the long way home…"

The afternoon had clouded over and the pickup was hot and humid. All three men were perspiring and Khamhuck was in an ill mood. He cursed the weather, angry with himself for killing the police officers. Of course, they hadn't given him much choice… He thought of the officer he had left in the ditch and wondered if he was still alive.

"We got them both, didn't we?" Khamhuck asked.

"Got who?" Soud asked. "We could have had a quick lunch at the Wildlife… I mean—"

"The police officers, you idiot!" Khamhuck shouted.

"You got them," Chur answered.

"Do you think they're both dead? The first one I shot—"

"I saw his body roll off into the ditch," Chur assured him. "No sign of life. Just a bag of bones tumbling down the hill."

"Even if he wasn't dead when we left him," Soud interjected, "he's sure as hell dead now. You shot him clean in the chest. He was bleeding out. He'll be as dry as a walnut by the time they find him."

All this reassurance was adding to Khamhuck's anxiety instead of allaying it.

"Pull off the road," he told Soud. Soud veered to the shoulder and slammed the brakes.

Khamhuck stepped out, took his cell phone out of his pocket, and told the men to wait in the truck while he made a phone call. He walked ahead until he was sure he was out of earshot and then dialed Touy's office.

"We need to talk," Khamhuck said.

Touy heard Khamhuck's voice and knew something was wrong. Khamhuck knew never to call unless it was an emergency. He would sit and wait for the call or to hear back. He had never had a problem with him before.

"Boun Souk Bar, tonight at ten," Touy said.

They both hung up.

Khamhuck returned to the truck. "Let's stop in town," Khamhuck said. He was thinking of those two cruisers that they had seen speeding to the scene. "We can get some lunch."

"Would have been better to eat at the Wildlife..." Soud mentioned.

Khamhuck gave him a look like he was about to murder him. Soud started the engine.

THEY sat down and ordered food at a roadside restaurant just on the outskirts of the town. When the waiter brought their order, Khamhuck put on his casual air, and without really looking up, already picking at his food, asked the waiter if he had heard anything.

"What's all the commotion here in town?" he asked. "Two police cars near damn killed us on the way here. We were just rolling, taking in the countryside and they come barreling at us one hundred an hour, all sirens blaring... Nearly gave my poor friend here a heart attack."

The waiter pursed his lips cynically as if had already seen it all. "Don't know," he said. "Something about some accident. Traffic jam on the road..."

He turned to return to the kitchen and a man at the table next to them who had overheard said, "It's no accident... I just came from there. I saw them carry the bodies of two police officers from the ditch into an ambulance. They had been shot by drug gangs. One was already dead I think. The other was rushed to the hospital."

"Well, I guess the road won't be clearing up anytime soon then," Khamhuck said, as though that had been his only concern.

"Guess not," the man replied and returned to his food. He ate quickly and left shortly after. He glanced continually in his rearview mirror as he made his way down the road. There had been something in those three men he didn't like. The other two barely looked at him, while the one who had spoken seemed to be trying too hard to show no reaction. He knew too, from the way they sat and ate together, that they weren't friends or colleagues or anything like that. They were more like the mountain wolves from the north, who run in packs, behind the leader of the pack. He shouldn't have said anything to them about drug gangs... Now, he just wanted to get home and make sure he wasn't followed.

❊❊❊❊

THE Boun Souk was a busy spot, a favorite with both the tourists and locals. It stood in the heart of the city of Luang Prabang facing Mount Phousy, with the Namkan and Mekong rivers flowing behind it.

Khamhuck and his men had parked the truck.

"We shouldn't have taken this delivery job in the first place," said Soud, as he shut the driver side door.

"Shut your mouth!" Khamhuck ordered. "You want to run the business, eh?" Khamhuck pulled his shirt back to reveal the pistol in his waist. "I'll blow your rotten head off. You hear me? Try me..." he growled, gritting his teeth.

Then Khamhuck stopped at the front doors and turned around to his men. "Keep your mouths shut in there. Let me do the talking."

Soud and Chur nodded.

The bar was dark inside. There was dim, low lighting and all the furnishings were made of a dark, brown hardwood. On the second floor were rooms that customers could rent by the hour. Touy was sitting at one of the long tables, with six men around him at the same table and another group at the table next to his. Khamhuck hadn't expected there to be so many men with Touy and it made him uneasy. Finally one of the men sitting next to Touy gestured for them to take a seat.

"I don't think I heard you clearly on the phone," Touy said once they were seated. "What kind of trouble did you get yourselves into again?"

Khamhuck looked around the table at the men's faces. Everyone was waiting to hear what he had to say. "We shot and killed two police officers," Khamhuck said matter of factly.

"I see," said Touy without looking up. "That's a terrible thing to do, killing police officers.... Very serious crime. Why would you do a thing like that?" Touy asked, looking up at Khamhuck for the first time. "Don't you know that the police in the area work for us? For me? You're lucky, they were from Nambark. If those two were mine, I would kill you right here."

"We had the boxes in the back seat of our pickup when they stopped us," Khamhuck explained in his defense. "They were searching the truck. They were going to find them."

"So, you thought the best thing to do would be to kill them?"

"I'm not sure they're dead."

"Even better!" Touy said. "Couldn't even get *that* right!" Most of the men let out a low chuckle. "Well… you'll be glad to hear, they're both dead now. One was killed on the spot, and the other died in on the way to the hospital."

Khamhuck let out a breath of relief.

"Lucky, eh?" Touy scoffed.

Khamhuck nodded slowly. "It was stupid…" he began.

Touy was suddenly on his feet. He was leaning over Khamhuck, furious. "What exactly was stupid?" he seethed.

Khamhuck hesitated. "*I* was stupid."

Touy sat back down. "That's right. The only stupid here are you three," he said, looking at them. "Not Yeen and not the policemen who were only doing their job. Next time you're stupid enough to get caught, you stay stupid. You let yourself get taken in and you keep your mouth shut. You let us handle the police. Suddenly you think you're smart? Smart enough to make a decision to take out two cops?"

Chur and Soud looked at each other. Soud was about to open his mouth to say something when Khamhuck kicked him.

"You're going to make up for this," Touy went on.

Khamhuck put on a false smile. He knew this was coming. "I think that's fair. What do you want us to do?"

"Simple job… Remember the Pathavongs? That house you took down? Well they had a son in Canada. He's here now and causing trouble for everyone."

Khamhuck nodded that he understood. "What kind of trouble?"

"Well, you know, he's a university man, living in the West, comes back here from Hollywood, with big ideas about justice and law and order and how things should be."

The men around table laughed. Touy carried on.

"He's been asking questions, saying he wants to bring his family's murderers to justice. Now… correct me if I'm wrong, but that would be you three, wouldn't it?"

Khamhuck, Chur and Soud all looked at each other.

"So you see?" Touy added. "This is your problem, too. I'm doing you a favour."

"It's a loose end," Khamhuck broke in. "We didn't know they had a son, abroad. We'll take care of him."

Touy shook his head slowly. "Still stupid…" he said. "He's a foreigner now. A Canadian, I hear. What do you think would happen if he turned up dead? There's enough heat on us with two dead cops. A dead foreigner right now would be really bad for business."

"What do you want us to do with him?" Khamhuck asked. He was growing tired of being called stupid.

"Find out who he's been talking to, first. I want to

know what he's been up to. Then take him out to the woods. Put a gun to his head. Tell him he's got twenty-four hours to leave town or get buried next to his family. Make sure no one sees you. Keep it quiet... Am I clear?"

Khamhuck nodded and got up. Chur and Soud followed.

"And one more thing," Touy said. "It'll make things easier if you gave the truck a new paint job. Go see Deuan. Get a new license plate, too. Just in case. He already knows you're coming."

* * *

DEUAN was sitting on his favorite chair. He spat when he saw Khamhuck walk in. "Park your bloody truck there in front of the metal scraps," he said, pointing to the pile.

Khamhuck directed Soud to back up and park as he had been told. Khamhuck tried to keep himself calm to avoid a conflict. He was fairly certain that Deuan knew who he was. Deuan had been working for Touy for awhile now after all, so he knew Khamhuck was a leader of a crew and should be shown respect. Khamhuck in the meantime, knew all about Mr. Deuan. Known to his employees as the ugly man in town. His features—short, bald, small ears, round face and dark skin, all lent him the look of an Indonesian orangutan they said. The rumour was that he was so ugly, his parents abandoned him when he was a child...Then there was the story of how he got the business. He started off as an employee, hired by the man who had taken pity on him. He could use the help, he said. He had a down-syndrome daughter that he needed to take care of now that his wife had passed away, and the extra set of hands would lessen the burden. A year later, at seventeen, the girl was pregnant. Her father went about trying to kill Deuan with a hammer. He found out he had been sleeping with her all that time.

They say he used to take her out for ice-cream. They were spotted on the street hand in hand and everyone knew something was going on except the father. Even the children knew. There was one particular scene no one ever forgot. After they had finished their cones, Deuan licked her mouth clean with his tongue. Children, playing on the street took to it at once, following them about chanting and asking them to suck each other's tongue which they seemed happy to do for them. That same day, on the way home, they went into an old shed where the girl's father kept junk furniture. Deuan started undressing her, telling her it was a game and that they would do things to each other for points. When the children asked her why she and Deuan weren't going for ice cream anymore she told them it was because they had a new game they played in the shed that she liked very much. Then one morning, her father found her vomiting. He though she might be sick and took her to a clinic. It hadn't been long after her examination. They ran a blood test and the nurse returned and told them she was pregnant. That's how the father found out. Deuan was forced to marry her and after her father died, he inherited the business. The place had grown in his hands, and business now was good. They were doing body work for all kinds of vehicles these days, not just stolen ones that they were disassembling for parts or transforming before returning them to market. The place was controlled and protected now by the Silavong Real Estate Company, controlled of course by Touy's father.

ONE of the younger employees gave Khamhuck the keys. He took them to the black Hyundai Accent parked next to the door.

"We will let you know when your truck is ready," he said.

They drove back to the hotel. As the three men walked up to the second floor, Sithana passed them on the stairs while on his way down to the bar for breakfast. He glanced at them, and they glanced at him.

"The guy looks foreign," Chur pointed out.

Khamhuck nodded. "That's him."

IT was a sunny day. After breakfast, Sithana called for a rickshaw and went to visit the museum at the former royal palace. On the ride and then in the museum, his mind was drifted to thoughts of his family and especially his mother. It was nearly this time of year, after harvest, that he usually came to the city with her to the market. Suddenly, he felt lonely. He thought of Viengvilay and wished she could be with him there, though he knew it would be unwise to be seen with her in public any more than they already had. He would see her tonight at the hotel, if everything went according to plan.

Then, coming out of the museum, he thought he caught sight of the same three men he had crossed at his hotel that morning. He didn't know if he was being paranoid or if he was being followed. His mind was in a haze.

He decided to take lunch by the river at an outdoor table with a view of the crowded street. If he was indeed being followed, then he would certainly catch a glimpse of them. Meanwhile, he watched as a host of sparrows feeding on the ground at his feet, flew up to the branches above each time someone walked by. He could hear them chirping and it seemed to him, they were content. He remembered how he used to be content in that way, a long time ago, when he was still a boy and this restaurant was a spot reserved for bicycle parking. Now there were food stands all along the river shore, and sitting there, he could see crowds of tourists. He was now in some way, a tourist himself, though he had grown up here, and maybe even felt a little ashamed for having left, for having abandoned everyone. He didn't have the heart to do it again... But what if he was indeed being followed by those three men? They knew the hotel he was staying at... Was it safe for Viengvilay to visit? He was about to call her when his food arrived.

❋❋❋

IT was late in the afternoon by the time Sithana returned to the Phousy Hotel. He hadn't seen those three men again, nor anyone that appeared to take any particular interest in him and he was beginning to think that fear and paranoia had gotten the best of him. Now, he was glad he hadn't called her to cancel. All he could think about was being with her later that evening.

He took a shower, changed and got ready for his date with Viengvilay. She had told him she would be there by six. By five-thirty, Sithana was already dressed and shaven and with nothing else to do but wait for her. It was now six-fifteen and he was still sitting on the edge of the bed, looking out the window, waiting… trying not to give in again to fear and paranoia.

"I'm not worried. I'll wait until six-thirty," he told himself. "Then I'll call and make sure everything's okay."

He thought that her parents might not have let her come. It was now seven-thirty and his cell phone was not ringing. He checked the wall clock again and then heard someone knocking at the door. He put the phone on the nightstand and opened the door.

"I'm sorry, I'm late… I had an argument at work," she said as he opened the door.

Sithana was elated. He took her up in his arms, lifting her off her feet. "I'll never forgive you for this!" he said, setting her back down.

"For what?" she asked, smiling and straightening her dress.

"For making me wait so long," he told her.

"You can wait," she said, smiling. "It might do you some good… I've been waiting for you for over ten years. Do I complain?"

"You know what they say, if you love someone…" Sithana began.

"Then you can wait all your life," she finished with a laugh.

She took out a box of rice, BBQ chicken, and a small container of chili sauce and then went into the washroom to change from her Laotian traditional dress to a denim skirt and t-shirt.

THEY lay next to each other in bed. Sithana was surrendering to the growing affection he was feeling for Viengvilay. Besides all the help and effort she had taken on his behalf, he was moved by the risk she was taking for his sake.

"I want to be with you every day," he said.

"Do you Sithana? So do I..."

"It won't be easy, but we can do it if we work together. Right now, I need to finish what I came here to do. I don't want you to give up on me, on us," he replied.

The city was still asleep at four in the morning when Viengvilay was getting ready to leave. "You need to be careful," she said, as she got dressed. "He wants to make you disappear. Wherever you go, call me, and don't go back to the village yet. I will let you know when it is safe."

Sithana who was watching her getting dressed, lay back down on the bed smiling. "I think you just want to keep me hidden away here for yourself."

Viengvilay jumped atop him half-dressed. "You think this is a joke?"

"I know, I know," Sithana conceded. "In the meantime, tell my aunt not to worry about me."

"She knows…"

"What about my uncle Ken?"

"I think it's best to keep him out of it for now," Viengvilay suggested, uncomfortably.

Sithana observed her closely.

He walked her out to the front doors and stood watching as she disappeared down the main road.

Alone in his hotel room, Sithana kept thinking about her and hoped she would get home safely. In bed, unable to sleep, he wondered what she had meant by keeping Ken out of it. His uncle's behavior had been troubling him for a long time and he felt it was time now to get to the bottom of things. Sithana knew that his family's land had come to them from his mother's side. Sithana's grandparents had three offspring, two girls and a boy. After the boy was killed in the war in 1972, they signed over all they owned to their eldest child, Sithana's mother… But Ken had argued for years that it was Sithana's father who asked the old man for the property on behalf of the entire family so they could work and live off it together. Sithana's father never made an official document for the share, but allowed Bouy and Ken to work on the land as agreed. Now that the family had passed and Sithana had emigrated, Ken argued that the land was more his than anyone else's. Viengvilay's father knew the story well and probably told her about it. Sithana remembered occasions when Ken appeared hostile towards Mr. Vilavan. He cut him off whenever he'd talk about land as he often did with aunt Bouy. Sithana was beginning to suspect that his uncle had already sold the land to the Silavongs. Why else would they have stopped harassing the family? How else did he get the money to rebuild the house?

HE must have fallen asleep after all. It was late morning when he heard the knock on the door. The knocks first came as blows from a hammer in his dream and then when he opened his eyes, from the door of his hotel room. He got to his feet groggily, went to the door and still half in a dream, without thinking, opened it.

Khamhuck was inside in a second. Chur and Soud followed next as Khamhuck knocked Sithana to the ground.

"Get your fucking face on the floor! Do it! Do it!" Khamhuck shouted. He put his foot on Sithana's head while Chur bent down and pressed his gun to Sithana's ear.

On the ground with the weight of the men on him, Sithana struggled to breathe as he heard someone dragging a chair closer to him. The heavy boot on his head felt like it could crack his skull at any time.

"I don't want to know about you," he heard a voice say. "I don't want to hear about you. Hell, if I have to look at your face again, I'm gonna cut it off like those Indians do in your country… So listen to me…" the voice said and the boot pressed a little harder. "You're going to leave this hotel and then you're going to leave this city. You're going to go the airport and you're going to leave this country." Khamhuck took his boot off Sithana's head. "If you don't, we'll make you disappear some other way. Do you understand me?" Khamhuck took a step back and kicked Sithana hard in his stomach. "Just like they did with your family… without a trace! Get me?"

Sithana could no longer take it when he realized that this was the same gang that had murdered his family. He twisted out of Chur's grip and turning face up, kicked Soud in the groin. Soud fell off, while Chur tried to hit Sithana in the head with the butt of his gun, but missed. That's when Khamhuck reached for the lamp on the nightstand and smashed it over Sithana's head, knocking him out.

SITHANA woke up later in his hotel bed. The hotel owner's wife was sitting on the edge of his bed, leaning over him, dabbing a wet towel on his forehead and muttering to herself.

"You are okay, now." she said, when he opened his eyes. "I am Noy Panya, and this is my husband Suriya Panya. We are the hotel owners. We found you lying on the floor. The other guests said there had been a fight."

"We don't want any fights in our hotel…" Suriya said, suspicious of Sithana.

"Oh, shush husband! Anyone can see, this poor man's innocent."

"In all my days," Suriya said, "I've never seen an innocent man covered in so many bruises."

"Well, you should get out more!" his wife retorted. "Come let's fix you some breakfast," she said to Sithana, "and you can tell Suriya and me, what's happening."

Sithana told the young couple his story and was surprised to know that they had heard of his tragedy and had known his family.

"Your father was a good man," Suriya told him. "He helped us when the drought came."

"Aiy Sithana," Noy said. "We know what happened to them. We want to help."

Sithana shook his head. "No, I can't…"

"You have two options," Suriya said. "Either you let us help, or you leave now and never do what you came here to do."

"We'll find you a safe place to stay," Noy added.

They were in the hotel dining room now. The room

was empty of guests. In the center was a dining table and around the wall was a counter. On top of the counter were cabinets for plates, coffee and tea cups… At the end was a white cabinet. Noy went over to it and removed a first aid kit.

"You cannot rent any hotel rooms in this city," she said as she tended to his wounds.

"You can stay with us on the farm until the funeral is over or I can take you to the airport… as you wish."

Sithana weighed his options. There was no way out, he thought. If he stayed, he would get killed. If he left, he would never have his family's remains buried in the village cemetery and, most importantly, he would never see Viengvilay again.

"I need to make a phone call," Sithana said.

"Of course, you can use the front desk."

Sithana dialed Viengvilay's number. "Listen, I'm leaving the hotel," he had told her. He assured her everything was okay, but she could tell from his voice something was wrong.

"Why?" she asked.

"I can't tell you now," he answered. "But I'll be at a farm a little ways out of town. I'll call you and let you know where I am as soon as I'm there."

He put the phone down. He never thought that Viengvilay would get into any kind of trouble.

A HALF-HOUR or so after she spoke to Sithana, Touy called her.

"I want to let you know, your friend is gone," he said.

"What did you do to him?" she asked.

"Nothing, my men told him to leave town or face the consequences. They just left my office a few minutes ago. Unfortunately, one of my men got shot. It's not good that a foreigner is carrying a weapon," Touy said.

"He's carrying a weapon? You must be kidding me," she said in surprise.

"Why are you surprised?" Touy asked.

"I just am," she said.

"You must know him well," Touy said and she became silent.

Touy yelled at her a couple of times, but she pretended not to know anything about the matter.

"Where did he go?" she asked.

"They told me they sent him to the airport. He should have arrived in Vientiane by now and be waiting for his flight back to Canada," Touy said.

"I would like to see you this coming weekend," he added.

"It's not a good time for me," she replied.

"Why?" Touy asked.

"As you know, I know his family well and I promised

his aunt I would help with the funeral. But since that plan is not going to happen and you just told me her nephew is gone, I can't just tell her to forget about it. I need to be with her and help her understand the situation. The most important thing is how to ask her to get her money back from the buffalo owner she bought for the funeral and send the animal back since there's no need. I'm sorry, I hope you forgive me and we can talk soon," she said.

"I understand. Do what you need to do and let me know if you need anything," Touy said.

"Thank you. I might need your help for money," she said to appease him.

VII

SURIYA and Sithana were standing by Suriya's motorbike. It was covered in red dust.

"We'll be on a dirt road within two minutes," Suriya said. "Down the old buffalo trail. Trust me… no one will come looking for you there."

The village of Ban Huoi Heen, stood between the high mountain gaps of eastern Luang Prabang, about thirty kilometers from the city, though it seemed longer because of the poor road conditions… and the motorbike which could only go at certain speeds which Sithana, who was trying his hardest not to fall off of, was thankful for. Some people preferred living in the villages. Life was simpler and cheaper. They grew their own food and didn't have to pay taxes or rent or electricity. The government barely knew they existed and the villagers liked it that way. They lived the old ways, free of outside interference. Though Suriya and Noy moved to the city years ago, they distrusted city-folk and still returned to the village at least every week end, always bringing their homegrown food back with them.

It was late afternoon, by the time they made it to

the village. The blazing sun was now blocked by higher mountains and the temperature was getting colder. Sithana had forgotten how cold a winter afternoon could be in the mountains of eastern Luang Prabang. He had only brought summer clothes.

They pulled up to a small house by a field and an old woman came out the front door upon hearing the motorcycle. She walked right up to them, kissing Suriya on the cheek and taking hold of Sithana by the arm.

"Have you boys eaten?"

"Yes, we had lunch," Suriya said. "This is my grandmother," he told Sithana.

The old lady walked them both into the house where they sat in the living room on the wooden floor.

"Grandma, this is my friend Sithana," Suriya explained to her. "Sithana might stay with us for a couple of days... or a week." He looked at Sithana. "Maybe longer..."

The old lady was missing some teeth, did not answer but smiled her vacant smile, and ignoring her grandson, began telling Sithana about the land in the area and how he should marry a girl in the village and work the land. "We need young people here," she said.

Sithana smiled.

"Who are your people?" she asked. "Do I know them?"

"My family are from Ban Boumxieng on the other side of the river," Sithana told her.

"Oh, Suriya's grandfather came from there, from Ban Boumlou. I know where it is," she smiled and laughed. "You see many a girl from our village have taken Boumxieng men for husbands."

The house was filled with children before long as they went on talking. Suriya suggested that he take Sithana for a walk outside and show him the rice field. The fields were about a couple of hundred feet wide but long and stretched to the foot of the mountains as far as they could see.

"Do you still remember how to plant rice?" Suriya asked.

"I do. I used to go to the field with my parents and work all day during school breaks," Sithana was telling him, when an old man came walking up the fields toward them.

"That's my father," Suriya said.

"Ah, there you are, son," the old man said, as he came up to them. "Who's this?"

"This is Sithana, he's from Ban Boumxay, on the other side of the Kong."

"Ah... Do you farm?" he asked Sithana.

"No, I don't...I..."

"Dad, Sithana comes from Canada," Suriya explained.

"What is that?" the old man asked. "Never heard of such a village."

"It's a country very, very far away. He came to visit family."

"Oh, well… another country, you say? Well, do people there eat like us?" he asked Sithana.

Sithana smiled. "Yes, of course."

"Well come inside and sit down for supper, mister come-from-a-country-very-very-far-away… I'm hungry."

Suriya and Sithana both smiled at the old man's caustic invitation and all were in a jovial mood when Suriya's younger sister brought food and put out a plate on a large vine tray on the floor for each of them. Suriya's father continued talking about his land, and everyone fell silent and listened as the head of the family spoke. Sithana could not keep his thoughts away from Viengvilay.

※※※※

SITHANA had given Vienvilay directions on how to get to Huoiheen Village. She had heard of the place before, and knew that if she left home at nine in the morning, she should have arrived there well before midday. She planned to spend the whole afternoon there with Sithana. They had the funeral to plan and decisions to make.

She knew a short cut and arrived in the village before midday as she thought. The village was quiet at that time of day as the children were in school in the next village, and most adults except for the elderly were working; some in the fields and many of the younger men in the city.

Sithana heard the sound of a motorbike and went to the front door to have a look. Viengvilay saw him and though they wanted to rush into each other's arms, they knew they couldn't. They didn't even hug, as it wasn't the norm, but just stood there, talking painfully to each other before being ushered inside the house by the owner.

"Bring your friend inside," said the old woman.

Sithana looked at Viengvilay and then the old woman. "We were thinking of going for a walk," he said.

The old woman nodded in agreement. "It is a beautiful day for it."

"I will show her the creek and the rice fields…"

"Good, good… My grandson is not here," he said to Viengvilay. "He will come home soon for lunch. You can meet him then."

But Sithana had already stepped off the porch. "Thank you so much…" he said. "But please don't wait for us. Viengvilay brought food for the two of us."

"We were thinking of having a picnic," Viengvilay said.

The old woman smiled.

Sithana and Viengvilay began making their way down the road.

"Thank you for having Sithana, here," Viengvilay

shouted, turning back.

Below the village was a long trail to the creek they took to get to the other side to the foot of the mountain. After a few minutes, they reached a bit where taller trees had shaded the trail, making it somewhat more comfortable for walking. Sithana couldn't wait any longer. He turned and embraced Viengvilay passionately.

They sat on a large fallen tree trunk and had lunch. Viengvilay told Sithana about Touy contacting her and what his men had told him about Sithana. Sithana wasn't all that interested and changed the subject.

"I have heard," he said, "that the President of the United States will visit Laos after the G7 summit in Japan."

"What does the summit have to do with us?" Viengvilay asked, a little annoyed.

"Nothing maybe… but if the United States provides funding for development, I think a portion of the money would pay for the cost of the corruption investigation. And you know what? We have an opportunity to proceed with our plan. Touy will be laying low that that day. Too much security, too many soldiers and police about securing the place for the president's safety."

"Right, so you believe they will?"

"It's not that I believe, it was announced on the radio and in newspapers a few days ago."

"Okay, I can see that it makes sense for hold the funeral

that same day. But I'm not sure the government is going to do anything about cleaning up all the corruption, just because of the summit. The government officials have been behind it all these years."

"Only the local government.... Listen, I read a study that showed that only 40% of the forest was left for logging. Sixty percent is gone, cut by illegitimate private foreign companies, mostly Chinese and Vietnamese. Local government authorities from all sectors, including the police, are taking bribes and allowing the loggers access to many areas of the forest. Many of the top officials are huddled together, creating their own circle and consolidating their power. We need money and help from other countries with the power to stop this type of illegal activity."

"But why would the US want to get involved?" Viengvilay protested.

"You may not believe it, but in Canada and the US, they take alot about the wars here... You know that since 1991, the US government has been trying to cooperate with the Laos government to find the remains of service men and women who went missing during the Vietnam War. There's a new effort underway again. The United States will fund the cost, some ninety million dollars I heard. They will be looking for the remains of their soldiers in the old battlefields... all up and down our village and the lands around it. The government will have to clamp down on criminals in the area. Not just Luang Prabang, but Oudomay, too."

Viengvilay was shaking her head. "Maybe if you lived here," she said. "You'd understand... They only way to stop them is if we all fight them together."

"If I lived here?" Sithana echoed.

Viengvilay smiled. "If you lived here, we could help the government arrest the criminals, you and I..." She pressed herself to him and kissed his cheek. "We would be hereos..."

Sithana looked down. A shadow seemed to fall over him.

"I don't think you will ever live here, again," she said, pulling away. "Why would you? You will be back in Canada soon, to your life and I will spend my days thinking about you and wondering where you are."

He lifted her chin with a finger until their eyes met. "You won't have to think about me... Do you know why?"

She shook her head.

"Because you will see me day and night for the rest of our lives," he said, looking into her eyes.

She smiled, and then they were silent. The sun was halfway up the mountains and the whole valley was in shade. The dropping afternoon temperature changed dramatically from hot to cool and breezy. He took her hand and together they walked back along the trail towards the village.

❊❊❊

VIENGVILAY returned home that evening and Sithana was left alone with the grandmother of the house. They were sitting in the kitchen. The old woman was tending to supper. By eight o'clock, with darkness enveloping the earth, the whole village was silent.

"You know," she said, "Fifty years ago, this place was a jungle. We used to come here just to gather food. The women picked wild fruits and berries and while men hunted for animals and set traps."

"What kind of animals were here back then?"

"Oh, all kinds, big and small...deer, turkeys, rabbit and much more... There no guns back then, so the men and women worked together to build traps to catch them. Some of the men preffered the bow and arrow. Some of the better hunters could even hit a running hare. That's how good they were," she smiling in recollection. "Suriya's grandfather was a very good hunter."

"Is that why you married him?"

She laughed and he could see that her upper teeth were gone.

"Not only that, he was a good man. He never let us go hungry," she said and then fell quiet as Suriya's father arrived home. He walked in muttering to himself, complaining about his son spending the night in the city. He threw his bag in the corner turning to his mother.

"Do you know your grandson won't be back until tomorrow?"

"Yes, he told me."

"He shouldn't have left you alone here."

"No, I'm not alone. I have Sithana here with me."

"Yes, I'm sure you've been regaling him with your tales," he said, and then turned to Sithana: "She repeats the same story to everyone she meets."

Sithana smiled at the man. He thought that perhaps it was the only thing she could vividly remember about her experiences, the love she had for her husband. It was obvious that she shared her past with everyone she met, and most importantly, it was something she didn't want to forget.

VIII

IT WAS eight days before the United States President was to visit Luang Prabang. Viengvilay and Sithana were planning to cross to the other side of the river by September 1st. The ceremony was expected to be held on September 2nd or 3rd, and as a result, all roads and bridges would be closed for the president's safety. Some regions in the province had already started to implement blockages and the army was moving personnel, tanks, and weaponry around. Checkpoints were also being set up. Sithana planned to take advantage of this time to re-bury the remains of his family, so that Touy's men wouldn't have the opportunity to terrorize the villagers and cause harm.

Meanwhile, Sithana's thoughts turned increasingly to Viengvilay. He began to worry about her safety, never thinking to worry about Noy's or Suriya's.

That morning Touy got a phone call from his contact at the airport. It was not the call he was expecting to get.

"What are you telling me?" he seethed. "He hasn't left?"

"No one on a Canadian passport has boarded any plane," the voice confirmed.

Touy got dressed quickly and called Khamhuck. "I want to see you right *now*!" he said.

TOUY was waiting, pacing around his office. When Khamhuck entered, he grabbed him by the neck.

"You...you lied to me." he said, gritting his teeth.

"I don't know what you're talking about," Khamhuck pleaded.

"You know damn well what I'm talking about. You lied to me about the foreigner... I *know* that he's never left town. You told me that he had gone to the airport, but I know for a fact that that's not true! I did you a favour, pulled you out of the trouble you made killing officers. Tell me why you lied!"

"Look, I wasn't lying. We sent him to the airport by taxi. I don't know how he got back to the hotel. Is he there now?"

"He's not stupid! Why even ask such a question? Of course, he's not there anymore! Who knows where he is now..."

"I'll take care of it," Khamhuck said.

"You bet you will!" Touy said, his voice low and serious. "First, go to the hotel and find out where Noy is. Find out what she knows. She knows something! She'll lead you to him. This time, make sure he leaves town. Put him on the plane yourself if you have to.

"Sure thing boss," Khamhuck said, nodding.

"Then, take these boxes to Viengvilay's school and

call me once you're done. Make sure his aunt doesn't go to Viengvilay for any help. I'll visit her after the United States President's visit to Luang Prabang, when the roads are open. And not necessarily to talk to her."

Khamhuck left the office, mulling over this latest bit of bad news to add to the pile of trouble that was mounting. This foreigner was causing trouble for eveyone. He was the sore spot and the thorn in everyone's side. Khamhuck would remove it once and for all. First, he'd have to get his truck back.

MR. Deuan was sitting near the counter as usual, but he walked away as soon as he saw them. He held the door for them, but didn't speak until they got closer and were almost face to face.

"There's your pick-up," he said gruffly.

Khamhuck had neglected to tell the garage the color he wanted on the truck. When he turned to look at it, his grey pickup had changed from grey to white, which he did not like. He shouted at Deuan, "I wanted black!" he said, hitting the countertop. "Who the hell asks for white?"

Deuan just smiled. "You didn't tell us what color you wanted," he reminded him. "Are we supposed to guess? I had a surplus of white..."

"I *did* tell you I wanted it black!" Khamhuck argued. "You just weren't listening to me."

Soud held Khamhuck back.

"You didn't mention anything about color," Soud said. "Remember? All you told him was to get it done as soon as possible."

Khamhuck scowled at Soud. "Damn it! Let's just go," he said. "Chur, you drive."

Khamhuck sent Chur to bring the truck to the front door while he and Soud approached the counter. They were expecting to pay the bill, but Deuan told them 'the boss' had called and told him not to bother charging them.

"It's your lucky day," he said.

Khamhuck detected the note of sarcasm in Deuan's voice. He also knew that if Touy wasn't charging, it meant it was no longer business; it was now personal.

Khamhuck and his men quickly collected the truck and headed back to the hotel. Touy had warned Khamhuck to keep a clean mind. Stay sober, he told him... Everyone knew Khamhuck and his men were on yama. Touy had told him specifically to lay off the pills, but before arrving at the hotel, Khamhuck's nerves got the better of him. Chur offered him a pill of yama, and they all took two before approaching the receptionist.

"I'd like to speak to Miss Noy Panya," Khamhuck said.

Noy hesitated, sensing something was off. She could

see it in his blood-shot eyes. "What do you want to talk about?"

"I'd rather speak in private," Khamhuck said, scanning the lobby.

Noy was reluctant, but before she could respond, Chur pulled out a gun and showed it to her. She quickly led them to the staff room, where they locked the door behind them.

Once inside, the three men focused their attention on Noy, waiting for instructions from Khamhuck.

"A simple question for you," Khamhuck began. "Where is the foreigner and don't pretend you don't know who I'm talking about!"

"We are a hotel… Many of our guests are—"

Khamhuck grabbed her arm before she could finish and shook her. "Don't lie to me!" he yelled. "Lie to me again, and I'll take you to see our boss. He won't be so kind! I know you treated him for his wounds that morning."

But Noy was tough. She had dealt with all kinds and in all states behind the hotel counter throughout the years. And then her life in the village often put matters in perspective. These city folk weren't half as dangerous as some of the men out in the bush. The bright lights and their filled bellies made them much softer than those men that appeared and disappeared without a trace in the bush.

"Oh, him… He left yesterday," she replied. "I don't

know where he is now."

"You cared a lot for him, to play nurse and treat his wounds… and after all that, you didn't ask him where he was going?"

Khamhuck looked around at his men. They all laughed sardonically.

He turned to Noy again. "You think you're funny? Making my men laugh at me, huh?" He shook her again. "Tell me where he went!"

"I don't know. He told me he wouldn't have time to buy a plane ticket to Vientiane. He asked me if I knew a place for a bus ticket. I told him where and how to get there. He looked scared and eager to get out of Luang Prabang."

Khamhuck turned to Soud and Chur. "That's what I told the boss…"

Khamhuck's men nodded at each other.

"Did he contact you after that?" Khamhuck asked Noy, relaxing now and letting go of her arm.

"No, but his aunt and a woman called me and asked the same question you did. They told me to let them know if he contacted me. They wanted to know where he is because his aunt is concerned for his safety. She wants to know if he's okay. I told her that he might have arrived in Vientiane by now and left the country already," she said, making up a plausible story. They seemed to believe her.

NOY watched them pull out of parking lot, making sure they were gone before calling Suriya.

"Are you okay, Noy?" he asked.

"I'm scared," she replied.

"I know. Make sure nobody sees you talking to me," he said.

"I will," she said.

A few kilometers from the hotel to the ferry, Soud was driving over the limit again, trying to get to the village school before noon. Police on motorbikes signaled him to pull over... but these were Touy's men. They must have not recognized the truck after its paint job. As the police took off their helmets and approached the truck, Khamhuck handed him cash. The policeman took the money, asked no questions, and waved them off. They continued driving to the shore and crossed to the other side. From there, it was another eight kilometers to get to the village.

Because of the delay at the crossing, they arrived at the village during lunchtime and Viengvilay, along with most of the children who generally ate at home, had already gone home for lunch. The three men went straight to the principal's office. He was eating at his desk and was wary of these men, but he spoke to them in a normal tone.

"What can I do for you?" he asked, wiping his mouth.

"Mr. Silavong sent some supplies for the kids," Soud said as he and Chur set the boxes down.

"Well, it's not the season yet, but thank you anyway," said the principal.

"The boxes are from him personally," added Soud.

"Thanks again, it's appreciated..." the principal ventured, not quite understanding.

"We have something for Viengvilay also," Khamhuck said.

"Ah, I see! Well if you leave it with me, I'll make sure Ms. Vilavan gets it..."

"We were hoping to give it to her personlly. It's from her fiancé. We have a message for her, also," Khamhuck added.

"Ah, well, she's gone home for lunch, you see, if you like, I can—"

"We'll see if we can't catch her at home, then," Khamhuck interjected. "You know things are about to get complicated soon with the presidential visit.. roadblocks, checkpoints..."

"I know," said the principal, smiling and trying to be affable. He watched them walk out of the building and enter their truck. They cruised down the street toward the village center, their windows rolled down, stopping everyone they met to ask if they knew whether the Pathavongs were holding a funeral; whether they knew someone who would do something as stupid as attend it; and most importantly, whether they had seen the foreigner, Sithana around. The principal watched, standing at his office window as each person they asked, answered with a shake of their head.

✳✳✳

SURIYA arrived at his home just before dusk, with Noy nestled behind him on their motorbike. Sithana was in the kitchen, engaged in lively discourse with the grandmother. But the mirth and jocularity quickly dissipated when Suriya entered, with a look of distress etched onto his face.

"People are looking for you in town," Noy spoke up. "This morning. The murderers of your family...three of them."

But Suriya intervened. "You can't be certain," he asserted.

"I'm sure it's them," Noy stated. "Why else would they be asking if he's still in the city?" She glanced over at Suriya, who then turned his gaze towards Sithana.

"It's a long road to proving their guilt," he told Sithana. "And we know we're talking about organized crime and corrupt government officials, not just a couple of thugs."

"It's everywhere!" the grandfather interjected. "Just today I heard on the radio $850,000 US dollars went *poof*... I'd tell you what we'd do them in my day!"

Sithana knew what the old man was talking about.

Close to a million had vanished from state funds in Xayaburi province alone. Senior executives from twelve firms were caught pilfering hundreds of thousands of dollars from government coffers. They listed phantom construction projects, illicit logging, purposely inflating expenses, bribing officials...The list went on.

"Were you followed?" Sithana interrupted. The idea had just struck him.

Suriya and Noy looked at each other. They didn't think so.

"All the same, I will start sleeping in the hut by the rice field. I don't want to put anyone in danger, more than I already have."

"Mmm, yes, smart..." mumbled the grandfather.

"Don't worry about us or my family," Suriya reassured him.

"I think it's best," Sithana said. "I'll be comfortable."

AS Sithana was laying down to sleep in the rice field, the stars still shone bright in the sky. He felt the cool night air and heard the countryside sounds, filled with the scent of plants and earth. He contemplated the serenity of the moment, and knew it wasn't destined to last.

He woke in the hut at six in the morning, just as the sun was beginning to rise, and the warm air turned hot and humid. It was late August, and everyone was keeping a watchful eye on their rice fields. The crops would soon be blooming for the next three months until their fields turned yellow, marking the harvest season in November. After that, they would plow the fields, turn the soil into mud, and plant rice again in June.

It was the first time in years that he recalled what his father had told him in the rice fields. It was back in September of 1998 when his father was plowing the field, and he had come down to help. His father had told him to stay with his mother, who was expected to give birth to his younger sister at any moment. His elder brother was with her, but their mother had asked him to go help his father in the field after he arrived. "Go help your father, Lium. Sithana will be with me," she had said in a soft voice.

Less than an hour later, Bouy's aunt had arrived from the north village and asked Sithana to go fetch the woman next door. "My mom," he said to the woman, but before he could explain, she had already understood. She took him by the arm, and they ran over together back to the house. He remembered watching his mother's face writhing with pain. Bouy then told him to go outside, where he passed several women who had come into the house to assist with the birth.

Sithana had been waiting outside for almost an hour. Then he heard a baby cry. He went in and saw someone take the baby from his mother, clean it, and give it back to her. He was fourteen at the time, and a few months later, he turned fifteen. He felt proud when he found out from his aunt that the baby was a girl named Dara, named a day after her birth by an older woman who was a good friend of his grandmother.

Dara was five years old when he left the country. She grew up with little memory of him, but his mother began telling her all about him as she grew older. When she turned twelve, she started writing to him often, sending photos and telling him how proud she was to have a brother. After Viengvilay returned to the village to teach at the school, she began sharing everything about him and his pictures with Dara. Viengvilay became not just a good friend, but a big sister to her until her death.

***

TOUY had asked Viengvilay to meet him at his office.

"Soon you'll be my wife," Touy said. "Have you thought about me at all?"

"Yes, and I don't have to," she said.

"Why's that?" Touy asked.

"Because we'll be together, unless something happens to me," she said, timidly.

Touy smiled at her innocence. "Did you get the gift?" he asked.

"Yes, thank you," Viengvilay replied.

"I wanted to talk about your friend Sithana," Touy said, moving in a little closer. "Can you tell me about him?"

"We were classmates in elementary school," Viengvilay said. "Then we lost contact when he left the country. I became friends with his little sister when she was twelve."

"With his sister only?" Touy asked.

"Yes," Viengvilay said.

"I see," Touy said.

"Before you and I got engaged, I invited him and my female friend who also knew him to my wedding," Viengvilay said. "We talked and joked, and he couldn't believe I was getting married."

"Did he ask about his family?" Touy asked.

"He did," Viengvilay said. "I gave him a newspaper article and told him to contact the police department for more information."

"What did he say?" Touy asked.

"He asked if it was worth it to know," Viengvilay said. "I told him it would make no difference and it was dangerous."

"And you want him to get a girlfriend here?" Touy asked.

"I'm not sure," Viengvilay said. "He's married to a

Canadian woman and has a child."

"Good talk," Touy said. "I love you."

Viengvilay tried to leave, but Touy pulled her arm back and kissed her. She freed herself. "I'll wait until our wedding night before we sleep together," she said.

Touy watched Viengvilay leave on her motorcycle. She pretended to care, but Touy knew better. He waved goodbye, smiling.

✳✳✳

VIENGVILAY was sitting at a small café next to the school, her purse resting on the table beside her. She pulled out her cell phone and dialed a number.

"Hey, it's me," she said when the line connected.

"Are you not teaching today?" came the voice of Sithana.

"No, it's my day off, but the principal wants to see me in his office," Viengvilay replied.

Sithana fell silent.

"Are you there?" Viengvilay asked.

"I'm sorry, yes, yes—I am here," he said after a moment.

"Don't worry, Sithana. Mr. Phommavong is a good man. "

Viengvilay explained that she was a half-hour early

for the appointment and was waiting at a café. She then recounted her conversation with Touy earlier that day, about their relationship and what she had said about Sithana's marriage. Sithana was anxious, but understanding.

Viengvilay rode the ferry back home and sat on a bench, reflecting on the story she had made up for Touy. She couldn't shake the feeling that Sithana might actually be married. As she arrived home, she broke down in tears.

Alone in the house, Viengvilay found solace in thoughts of Sithana, despite the complications and confusion that surrounded them. She took a short nap, too exhausted to hold on to her thoughts any longer.

Hours later, she heard the door open and knew it was her mother. "What's happened?" her mother asked, her voice laced with worry. "What are you doing in bed? Are you sick?"

"I'm fine, Mom," she said, getting up, staring out the window as the sky grew darker. "I'll come down in a moment. I'm fine... just tired."

"Okay, well, I'm making your favourite today," she said. "It'll be ready soon."

Viengvilay straightened up the bed and followed her mother out of the room. Her father had already arrived and was waiting at the table for his supper. He noticed his daughter hadn't been working again. He waited until after supper to confront her.

"Is something wrong, Viengvilay? Are you pregnant?" he asked, after he had satisfied his hunger.

"I'm fine, Dad," she replied, her hair falling loosely around her face.

"Ah, leave her be," his wife said.

"I'm just wondering… since she's not gone to work. Maybe she's pregnant…"

"How can you say such a thing! Foolish man!"

Her father shifted in his seat. "I may be foolish," he admitted. "But I know how to count at least. Since that boy arrived from that ice country of his, you've missed work more than three times. I warned you about getting involved with the Pathavongs," he said, now pacing around the room. "You might not know this, but Ken and I have been working for the Silavong family for a long time now. Before the Pathavong fire, even. Ken knows exactly what happened and why. You don't think he's watching and listening every day to that boy? Are you hearing me? Stop seeing him!"

Viengvilay sat beside her mother, avoiding her father's gaze and fighting back the tears.

Later that night, Viengvilay was on her bed, all cried-out and staring at the ceiling in disbelief, when her phone rang. She answered, relieved to hear from Noy. They talked briefly, and Viengvilay felt a glimmer of hope that things might work out in the end.

AFTER ending her talk with Viengvilay, Noy hit the button once more to call Suriya when a passing truck caught her eye. Although it was similar to the one she saw days earlier, this one was white, not gray. It crept down the narrow back street and stopped briefly before speeding off after she had noticed it.

Inside the hotel, she discovered an unsealed white and blue envelope atop the counter. After opening it, she read the words scrawled on the paper inside: "Notify us if he contacts you. The boss will appreciate it." Two phone numbers were listed at the bottom, one of which belonged to a real estate agency situated in Namekan, a mere fifteen-minute drive from her workplace. She discarded the message at first but soon retrieved it, tore it up, and discarded it once more.

Her heart was racing. She couldn't sit still. A colleague found her pacing the hallway in a state of agitation. "Are you alright? Someone came looking for you," he said. "They left an envelope."

✳✳✳

SITHANA waited for Viengvilay's call, but his cell phone wouldn't ring or buzz no matter how hard he stared at it. Without Viengvilay's help, things would get tougher.

He wasn't sure what to do next. Talking to Suriya was pointless. Organizing the funeral and returning to the village was as difficult as catching an elephant barehanded. Meanwhile, he worried about Viengvilay's safety.

When Suriya knocked on the door, Sithana stood up from the chair. "Oh, grandma's not with you," said Suriya, smiling.

"She's at the neighbor's house," Sithana told him. He didn't feel like talking, but he knew it would be impolite to remain silent. Meanwhile, it seemed that Suriya, who was concerned about Noy's phone call, had something he wanted to tell him.

"Noy called me this afternoon. She'll be home soon and has something to tell you," Suriya said, looking at him.

"I've been waiting for Viengvilay's call," Sithana confessed, biting his lip.

"Some men came to the hotel looking for you. I think it's the same men that roughed you up the other day... They haven't given up."

"I'm grateful for your help," Sithana said.

Suriya nodded. "Give me a second," he said and left the room. He returned a moment later with a bottle of homemade rice whiskey.

"There's something else..." Suriya began. "I'll let Noy tell you more about it, but Viengvilay thinks your uncle

Ken might have been involved in your parents' death. Viengvilay says her father too, might know something. Poor girl was crying. I can't imagine how you both must feel!"

Sithana buried his face in his hands. Things were getting out of control. Noy and Suriya were accidentally getting involved in his situation. Now they were at risk and he was again forced to rely on their trust, knowing his life was somewhat in their hands. If the gang ever came for Noy, she might tell them about him, and he wouldn't leave the region alive.

The lights were on in every room. Sithana continued fretting and rubbing his neck, when they heard the sound of a motorcycle. A beam of light shone above the windows. All eyes turned to the door.

"Here she is," Suriya said.

Noy entered, no smile on her face, and went straight for Sithana.

"We need to talk," she said.

SITHANA alone understood the workings of his mind that night. He lay down, rose, lay down again, but slumber remained elusive. Perched on the edge of the bed, he steadied himself with both hands and gazed at the darkened wall.

The notion that Ken might have played a part in his parents' demise proved difficult to fathom. Since hearing of the long-standing land dispute between Ken and Sithana's father from Noy, Sithana had mulled over whether Ken possessed the mettle to undertake such a heinous act. Had Ken wedded Sithana's aunt solely for that purpose, devoid of any genuine affection? Such thoughts tormented Sithana, leaving him uncertain whether even his aunt had known of Ken's atrocities against her own sister and her family.

At 5:30, dawn crept over the hills and the sounds of the villagers slowly replaced the hush of the night. He couldn't stay in bed any longer. The owner of the house brought over heaps of food to the kitchen table: rice, fried eggs, smoked meats, chilies, and steamed cabbages, the scent wafting through every corner of the home. He ate with the family, uncertain of his place in their midst.

"We won't be back until Friday," Suriya stated. "But Noy will be in touch if we hear anything."

"Thank you, I appreciate it," he replied, twining his hands.

Suriya drove, with Noy sitting behind him. The mild morning sun trailed behind them as they traveled westward to the hotel. The heat hadn't yet arrived, and some stretches of the road remained in the shade. The morning seemed to carry remnants of the dawn.

Noy was working the morning shift from seven to

three this week. Since Suriya was staying in town with her, and he was doing odd jobs in the city to supplement his farming income, they would only be using his motorbike.

"Pick me up at three?" she reminded him, tapping his back as she hopped off the bike.

"At Viengvilay's?"

"No. She said she'd come see me here."

"At the hotel? You think that's smart?"

Noy gave Suriya a look.

"Okay…Okay. See you at three," he said before driving off. They had spoken on the subject before. Suirya felt they were doing enough by sheltering Sithana. He wasn't sure getting involved any deeper was wise or helpful. Noy, however, insisted that it was their moral duty.

THE morning shift flowed steadily, with mostly just the long-term guests around. The evenings, in contrast, buzzed with a constant stream of phone reservations and walk-ins before nightfall. Since Laos opened up to tourism in '91, Luang Prabang had become the prime spot for visitors, and even some of its poorer citizens saw a rise in opportunity and prosperity. Others however, mostly those without education or skills were easy pickings for organized criminals, like Touy Silavong, who lured them to work illegally.

Noy entered the dining room area to find Viengvilay scrolling through her phone, trying to verify the price of the diamond sent by Touy. They hugged warmly and then sat down to discuss Sithana's situation. Viengvilay had just told Noy about her dreaded suspicions that Ken might have been involved somehow.

"But how do you know for sure that Ken had something to do with Pathavong's killing?" Noy asked.

"I don't," Viengvilay admitted. "Not yet."

"You must really care for Sithana…"

Viengvilay broke out in tears. "I'm engaged… My father told me to stop seeing him… My mother…. My mother worries about me."

"But you won't stop seeing him?"

"It's not right!" was all Viengvilay could say.

Noy changed the subject. "This land dispute," she began. "It's in the Chompet district? I remember the government was giving it out to anyone who would settle it…"

But Viengvilay wasn't listening. "The day before they set fire to the house," she went on, "Touy called Ken to meet with him. At Park Mong! That's twenty-five minutes' drive. Why? The answer is obvious."

❋❋❋❋❋

About a year ago:

Ken was sitting in Touy's office.

"Map," Touy demanded, sliding a sheet of paper across the table to Ken.

"I can tell you," Ken replied.

"No. Draw it," Touy commanded, his eyes narrowing.

Ken's hand shook as he drew the map, but he finished and handed it to Touy, who studied it intently.

"Now listen carefully," Touy said, his voice low. "Your job is done, and you'll get half of the land. I'll take the other half and pay you for the pieces I want. I'll also pay to rebuild your house. How much do you want?"

Ken hesitated, then spoke. "I just want a good house for my wife and me to live comfortably in. And if you can, I'd like to work for your company until I turn seventy. For the land along the river, I ask for fifty thousand dollars. For the rest, I leave it to you."

Touy nodded, his face softening. "You won't get in trouble. What you said was fair. I'll take the lands on the other side of the hills and pay you. But I want to buy five acres by the river for three thousand dollars. It's for my future father-in-law."

※※※

NOY was now asking, "Is there any written contract?"

Viengvilay replied, "I don't know, but I don't think so." She added, "I'm not sure either, why Ken and my father went along with him so easily. As a matter of fact, this was even before Pathavongs were killed, and the land wasn't even Ken's!" Viengvilay spoke angrily.

Noy asked, "Did your father get his portion of the land?"

Viengvilay was ashamed. "Yes... I don't know... but I think so. I'm sure..." She fought back tears again. "But he won't build anything until I marry Touy...I think Touy has promised to build them an even bigger house there."

Noy asked, "And Sithana knows about all this?"

"I will never forgive him," Viengvilay went on, about her father. "To take the Pathavong's land. His brother-in-law... they were family!"

Viengvilay looked away in anger, thinking of Dara and their childhood friendship.

I X

BOUY hadn't seen Sithana in some time and she was growing concerned about her nephew. One evening, not being able to stand it anymore, she refused to eat supper and decided to confront her husband.

"The boy was causing nothing but trouble," Ken said. "I tried talking some reason into him, but no luck… I guess he's gone to Vientiane to find the gunman." Ken stopped chewing and rested his fork on the plate. "But everyone knows they already got him and he's dead," he said.

"How can you be sure the gunman is dead? They say there were multiple gunmen," his wife protested.

"Who are these 'they' that you're talking about?" asked Ken.

"The journalists," she said.

"What journalists? They don't know what they're writing about. They just want to sell papers, understand?" he said, raising his voice. "That's how these people make their living."

"But not just newspapers, TV, radio, and people at the market are talking about it, you know," she said.

"Mind their own business is what they should be doing. Let them say what they want. They don't know what they're talking about. It's not going to change anything.

The killer is dead," he said. "It's a fact everyone, especially your nephew, has to accept."

THE ferry was docked on the shore that Saturday morning, empty of passengers, when Viengvilay boarded. On week days, a long line of vehicles would be waiting to disembark. That morning, the ferry man just waved her in and she rode her motorcycle straight onto the deck. Twenty minutes later, she was donning her helmet again, riding up that red dust road to Sithana.

The village was quiet most afternoons. The young were in school, the adults were in town working and the elderly were napping. No one was in sight. Sithana had hidden Viengvilay's motorcycle inside the barn next to the house where the animals would go on hot days for shade and escape the heat. The smell of buffalo urine lingered. Viengvilay was used to it, but for Sithana, it was a little uncomfortable.

They had been talking about Sithana's uncle, Ken.

"Everyone knows my uncle's story," Sithana said.

"What do you mean his *story*?"

"You know... how before he married my aunt, he was a police officer... Then one day, he hit and killed a young girl while chasing a bicycle thief. They say he took off. He didn't stop for the girl he ran over and he didn't catch the thief either."

"I knew he had been a policeman, that he lost his job, but I—"

Sithana was nodding. "That's right. There was an enquiry and he was fired. He started working for the Silavongs shortly after. Who else? He said he was doing security for them, but he was another 'property negotiator' for the company... You know convince poor land owners, desperate for money, to sell their land for half the market value. Convince them by any means..."

Viengvilay's hands were shaking. "Now, they have my father doing the same thing..."

He took hold of her hand. "I've been wondering why Ken wasn't keen on having me in their house from the day I arrived," he said. "I know my aunt was very excited."

"Ken must feel threatened..."

"He must know something about what happened, if..."

"If what?" Viengvilay asked.

"If he's not directly involved somehow."

"You think?"

Sithana shrugged. "It's hard to imagine."

"You must be careful," she broke out. "If that's true, who knows what he might do? I love you, Sithana. I can't sleep at night for thinking and worrying about you. I can't imagine what would become of me if you left." She looked away.

Sithana leaned in to look her in the eyes. "I told you, didn't I?"

"You told me...?" she replied.

"I told you, I won't leave Luang Prabang without you," he said.

"I know, but..." she started.

"There's no 'but'," he said, cutting her off.

She turned and faced him, and he took her in his arms. With her face still on his chest, he could feel her breathing on him, his chin on her forehead. It felt as if they would never let go of each other.

VIENGVILAY arrived home just as the sun was setting. A white Toyota Highlander marked with "police" on both sides of the doors and a bar-red light on its roof was parked outside the house. She stopped and wiped the sweat off her forehead, her heart pounding with thoughts of what might have gone wrong with her parents. Two men came out of the house, neither of whom were wearing police uniforms. They stood at the doorway waiting, while Viengvilay parked her motorcycle on the side of the house. She approached them, taking off her helmet.

"Is anything wrong, officer?" she asked. "My parents—"

"They're fine. They're inside," said one of the policemen.

"Are you Viengvilay Vilavan?" asked the second.

"It's Sunday," Viengvilay said.

"Yes, but for special cases, there's no weekend," the first replied.

"Listen, young lady," the other interrupted. "We got an order from the district police chief to pick you up and bring you to the station."

Viengvilay scowled. "For what reason?"

"Not for us to say…"

Just then her father came bellowing out. "I told you!" he said. "I knew this would happen! I warned you."

"Please go back inside, sir," said one of the police officers. "There is no problem, I assure you. We just need to bring your daughter in for questioning."

Viengvilay said nothing. Her mother took her father's arm and pulled him back inside the house.

THE sign outside the station read "Police 472 Supanou Vong Street." The national flag fluttered on a pole taller than the building's roof. Beside the structure were many bamboo sets, displaying a mix of green and yellow leaves, suggesting both old and new growth.

The large waiting room was bare and empty, indicating that the station only opened on Sundays for special circumstances. The police officers escorted her to the office where the police chief sat waiting. He motioned for her to sit and shut the door before addressing her. He was dressed casually in a blue T-shirt and sandals, and didn't smile until she spoke.

"Why did you bring me here to see you?" Viengvilay asked. "You think because I'm a simple elementary school teacher that I don't know my rights?"

"Actually, someone usually does this, but it's Sunday as you know, and I couldn't get any of my officers to come in," he said, smiling. He picked up a folder from his left, opened it, and glanced down. "Why have you visited Phousy Hotel a couple of times since the foreigner arrived?" he asked.

"He's my childhood friend who returned home to bury his deceased family. I told him from the first day he arrived that I would help him with anything he needed. We were planning for the funeral... But then something went wrong. His uncle told him to leave. They said he was causing trouble here, so he grew afraid and left."

"Is that all that happened?" he asked, looking straight into her eyes.

"I'm engaged and getting married," she replied, meeting his gaze. "What are you implying?"

"Nothing, nothing... and congratulations," he added. "But do you love your fiancé?" he inquired.

"That's none of your business," Viengvilay retorted. "Who told you to ask me these questions?"

"You know who," he replied cryptically.

Viengvilay was fed up. "We both work for the government... We're supposed to serve. I teach and you're supposed to protect us, not pry into our personal lives," she exclaimed, her frustration boiling over. "Yes, we both know who! And you tell him, that what he's doing isn't right... And you! You should be ashamed of yourself!"

"I'm just conducting an interrogation..."

Viengvilay sneered in disgust. "Even before our engagement, he was already controlling me: sending someone to spy on me, following me everywhere I went, insisting I see him every day... and now this!"

"If that were the case, then it would only be because he cares about you. This foreigner is a dangerous man."

But Viengvilay wasn't listening or biting. "I get taken from my home... you police terrorize my elderly parents. I get treated like a criminal! Well... I'm afraid of him! You think he cares for me? I'm *afraid* of him. You're supposed to be protecting me!"

Studying her as he had been all this time, he knew it was no use. He closed the manila folder and put his pen away.

"I'm sorry you were treated this way. You've done nothing criminal, but you shouldn't be associating with this man who we believe has," he said and stood up. "I want you to keep what we discussed here today between us only," he added with a smile. "You're free to go."

DURING the drive, the police chief was debating what and what not to tell Touy about the interrogation. It frustrated him to think that they had asked her so many pointless questions when she hadn't done anything unlawful. He wondered how disappointed Tuoy would be at hearing the news. The chief knew that his disappointment usually led to an outburst of anger.

Upon arriving at Touy's mansion, a woman in a black apron opened the gate for him and gestured for him to drive inside. The chief parked his car and was once again struck by the grandeur of the estate. Situated on three acres of land the mansion looked out over the Mekong River. The landscape was constructed in the style of a northern Thai forest, with lower bamboo lining the six-foot high cement wall and soft Japanese grass covering the ground.

Touy was waiting for the chief in his parlour room. "So... what you got for me?" he asked.

"Nothing new... She says she was only trying to help him with the funeral; that your men scared him away and she hasn't seen him since."

"You believe her?"

It was a dangerous question. The chief knew he had to be careful in answering it.

"I think she's telling the truth about them being afraid. She's a tough young woman, but I think she's too afraid to cross you. She told me so."

Tuoy smiled. "She has no reason to fear me. Well, there's nothing I can do about that right now…. She can make her own decisions and think what she wants," Touy said.

"Of course, sir." the chief said. He didn't press the matter and answered the rest of Touy's questions as curtly as possible. He was desperate to end the conversation and get out of there.

As he left the mansion, the chief reflected on Viengvilay's interrogation. He couldn't shake the feeling that there was something more to her story than what was in the file and something Touy wasn't telling him. Then at home, the chief confided in his wife about the Viengvilay and Touy and the whole surreal proceedings. But his wife only berated him.

"So now you go about spying on women because of this man's jealousy?"

"She's engaged. She shouldn't be running about with that foreigner. It's unseemly."

"Ha! I'll tell you what's unseemly. A man your age being the lap dog of another man half your age. You disgust me!"

The chief was used to this sort of treatment from his wife. "I disgust you, eh? You want me to lose my job? Is that what you want? We'll see how much your fat tongue wags when we're all homeless."

※※※※

THE sun beat down on the windshield throwing off a glare that annoyed Khamhuck. It bothered him that they had been wasting too much time and money working for Touy, while his other men, even Deuan, paid them no respect. He should be importing goods from China instead, avoiding the mess with the police and men like Touy. He could be his own boss. He told himself, as he always did, that this would be the last time.

He dialed Touy's number on his cell. "It's me..." he told him when Touy answered.

"Meet me at the same place as last time in fifteen minutes," Touy said.

They waited outside for him. When Touy's Mercedes GLC finally pulled up next to them, Khamhuck step out of his truck and into it. From behind the tinted glass of his expensive SUV, Touy gave Khamhuck a new set of instructions.

"This is your last chance," he told him. "Don't fuck this up! Park the truck somewhere for a few days. I'll be sending some motorcycles with my guys. You can use those. Once the job's done, you can return the bikes, get in your truck and leave town for a couple of days. Got it?"

Touy drove away. Khamhuck stood watching until his SUV disappeared from view and then got in the truck and told Chur to head back to the hotel.

KHAMHUCK handed Chur and Soud helmets before they pulled off the lot and rode away on Honda 300 CC motorcycles. They barrelled down the main road towards the riverside. The busy traffic wasn't much of problem for their motorcycles. Weaving and swerving through the cars, they cut off anyone who was in their way, ignoring the angry motorists and the cursing and shouting they couldn't hear over the roar of their motorcycle engines anyway.

Bouy and Ken weren't home when they arrived. The neighbor heard their dog barking and came to the house. Khamhuck took off his helmet and spoke to the man.

"We've come to see Ken," Khamhuck announced. "Is he around?"

"They're in the field," the man said, as he walked off with a limp in one of his legs.

"Well, we need to see him," Khamhuck told the old man.

But age had made the man indifferent or deaf to other people's needs. He answered without turning around, raising a hand to point to the trail that rose up the hill. "Well you better start walking then. Your bikes won't make it up there."

All three men looked at the trail snaking up the hill and frowned. Khamhuck cursed.

He looked up and down the street. "I have an idea," he

said, when he saw a young couple across the road tending to their pig pen. They had their two boys with them, helping and carrying wood. Khamhuck approached the father.

"You know Ken?" he asked him.

The man nodded.

"I need to talk to him. I have message from his boss."

The man looked over Khamhuck at Chur and Soud, and Khamhuck could see that he was suspicious.

"Why don't you head back," Khamhuck told his men. "It's just a message, after all," he said, smiling at the man. "We don't all need to be here waiting."

Chur and Soud looked at each other, somewhat confused, but decided to do what they were told.

"Listen," Khamhuck said. "I'll give you five thousand kip if you have one of your boys go fetch him for me. I don't feel like walking up that giant hill. Not today." Khamhuck held out the money.

The man took the money and called for his eldest son. "Go fetch our neighbour Mr. Vilasak. Tell him there's someone here wants to talk to him." Then he turned to Khamhuck. "You can come back in half an hour," he said. He watched Khamhuck return to Ken and Bouy's house, where he took a seat on the steps. He turned to his wife beaming, flashing her all those bills. "That idiot!" he whispered to his wife and laughed. "Ken and Buoy are probably on their way back for lunch already."

The boy met them halfway from the village as the couple were making their way home for lunch just as the boy's father had said they would be. "There's a man who wants to see you," he told Ken, "He says he's got a message from your boss," and then ran back ahead of them.

"You keep quiet." he told his wife. Her heart pounded, fearing the worst for her nephew.

KHAMHUCK was half-asleep still sitting on the front steps when they reached the house. He rose to his feet when he saw Ken coming down the path. There were no handshakes and no greeting of any sort. Khamhuck was used to it. In his line of work, people would rarely have a reason to be happy to see him.

"Let's talk inside," was all Ken said as he passed him on the steps.

"I'll get right to it," Khamhuck said, once they sat down. "I'm here about your nephew. He's making trouble for everyone."

"We haven't heard from him since the day he left the hotel," Ken said.

"So you don't know where he is?" Khamhuck looked him in the eyes. "You want me to tell our boss that?"

"Well, it's the truth."

Khamhuck crossed his arms over his chest. "Well, that doesn't help anyone," he said. "I heard you were planning a funeral…"

"That's right. But it can't proceed without him. Once we know he won't be able to make it, we'll have to cancel the funeral," Ken said. "And this business is finished once and for all."

"I'm not sure the boss is convinced," Khamhuck said. He rose from his chair. "You better handle your part. As usual, we'd like you to let us know if your nephew contacts you or if you see him. I'll be back," Khamhuck said and walked out of the house.

Bouy was on Ken at once. "Why did that ugly man say 'as usual' to let them know? Have you been informing them about my family?" Bouy asked, red in the face. "Explain yourself Ken! Do you know how hard it has been to lose my sister? My niece? Oh, poor, sweet innocent Dara!" she cried.

Ken's words left Bouy feeling uneasy. She knew that their family was facing a difficult situation, but she couldn't understand why everyone felt threatened by Sithana. She went off to work in the garden alone for the rest of the working day, trying to calm her thoughts. As she worked, memories of her childhood and her sister, whom she had admired, came flooding back. She remembered how good her sister had been at tending garden. She and her sister had learned the value of hard work and the importance of taking care of the land from their parents.

She wondered if Ken truly loved her, or if he was only using her as a means to an end. She had always suspected that his intentions towards her family's land were not entirely pure. Now, with his words ringing in her ears, she felt more unsure than ever.

Bouy sat down on the ground and wiped her tears away with her sleeve. She knew that she couldn't let her emotions consume her. She had to stay strong for her family and for herself. She took a deep breath and resumed pulling out the weeds from her onion garden, as she spread the pile of chicken manure over the soil.

As she worked, she made a silent vow to protect her family's land and to honour her sister's remains and to not let anyone get in her way.

SITHANA was in the kitchen with the grandmother who was preparing chicken for the family lunch.

"Are you hungry?" she asked, plucking the freshly-slaughtered chicken. "We have plenty of food. Fresh chicken. They have a lot of meat on them this time of year. They've been feeding on the fields for months." she said smiling. Sithana stood there watching her, wondering why that made her so happy.

"So... Are you going to marry that girl?" she asked, looking up from her chicken briefly to catch his reaction.

Sithana smiled. "We'll see what happens."

"I mean, have you thought about it?"

Feeling like he should help her cook, Sithana pulled a stool from the corner and sat down next to her.

"It's hard to think of anything besides my family right now, but... yes, I have...Here let me help."

Sithana went for a walk after lunch along the creek, following the same trail he had taken with Viengvilay. His talk with the grandmother had made him pensive, and a little gloomy. Meanwhile, the early afternoon temperature was rising. Sweat was running down his back. The sun shone through the trees, and the sounds of insects singing were coming from all directions.

Arriving at a large coarse-sanded clearing by a ravine, tired and hot, Sithana took off his t-shirt and sat down on a boulder by the water. He thought of the man who had threatened him in the hotel room last week and was angry. "I will make you disappear without a trace, just like your family," the man had said. Still sitting, he picked up a stick from the ground. He aimed the stick at empty space, imagining the face of the man. He realized the man needed to be defeated. All men like him needed to be defeated. He swung the stick at the man's face, pushing it into his throat and screamed, his voice echoing far down the creek.

It seemed like all his strength had left him with that scream. He tossed the stick to the ground and broke down. Sitting on the sand, he tucked his knees in his arms. Tears poured down his face, mixing with the sweat.

As Sithana sat there, he knew this momentary weakness would soon pass. He had let his anger and frustration get the better of him. Yes, he couldn't help but feel a sense of satisfaction from imagining himself defeating his enemy and he realized that he needed to confront his fear and find a way to protect himself and Viengvilay.

Looking out over the water he saw a fish jump out of the creek. He watched it swim away, and then he noticed something else—someone moving in the brush.

Sithana got up to investigate. As he approached the edge of the woods, he heard a rustling in the bushes. He stopped, his heart racing, and then saw a figure step out onto the path. It was Viengvilay.

"I thought you might be here! I've been looking for you," she said, walking towards him. "Sithana, is everything okay?"

Sithana felt a wave of relief wash over him. "I'm fine. I just needed some time to myself."

Viengvilay looked at him, concern etched on her face. "Are you sure? You look like you've been crying."

Sithana wiped his face with his T-shirt. "I just needed to let some things out."

Viengvilay nodded, still looking at him. "Well, if you ever need to talk, I'm here for you."

Sithana felt a warmth in his chest. He had never had anyone offer him such kindness before. "Thank you, Viengvilay. I appreciate that."

Viengvilay smiled. "Come on, let's head back. I have something to tell you."

Sithana followed her back to the village, feeling lighter than he had in a long time. He knew that he still had a lot to figure out, but he felt like he wasn't alone in the journey.

They took a couple of steps and Sithana finally asked, "What did you want to tell me?"

"I've been thinking of how to start...I don't want to worry you. You have enough on your mind, I can see."

"Just tell me, Viengvilay," he pleaded.

Viengvilay took a deep breath and then just blurted it out: "They took me to the police station yesterday. They were waiting for me when I got home. They wanted to know if I had seen you and where you were."

"What did you tell them?"

"That I hadn't seen or met with you since you left the village."

"I don't like it," Sithana said. "I've made a decision. The moment before you showed up.... I have to put an end to this. They won't stop hounding us, ever."

Viengvilay was alarmed. "What are you going to do?"

"First, I'm going to rent a motorcycle, so I can get in and out of this village and go into town when I need to. You're risking too much coming here all the time. One day, they will follow you."

He had nothing to lose, he thought. He would have to confront them sooner or later—and it was better to confront them on his terms than wait around to be discovered. He remembered a rickshaw driver telling him that if the men were arrested, they wouldn't go to prison because their gang leader would pay to have them released and put back on the streets and into the workforce. What was the point of going to the police then? His one-week plan had been unsuccessful, if not naïve. Things had to move forward toward a resolution one way or another. They couldn't just get away with it.

They reached the fields and sat by the edge of the rice patties, observing the buffalos grazing. They had been sitting in silence for some time, when Sithana noticed that one of the buffalos appeared to be staring at him intently. He felt a strange connection to the animal, almost as if it was trying to communicate with him. He rose to his feet and approached the herd.

As she watched Sithana walk towards the herd, Viengvilay couldn't help but feel a sense of admiration for Sithana's determination to seek justice for his family. She knew that the path he had chosen was risky, but she also understood why he felt like he had no other option. She had seen the toll that the loss of his family had taken on him, and she knew that he couldn't continue living with the weight of their deaths on his shoulders. She hoped that they would be able to find some closure and move on from the tragedy soon. At the same time, Viengvilay couldn't help but worry about the potential consequences of Sithana's actions. She knew that violence would only lead to more violence, and she didn't want to see him get hurt or worse.

As Sithana neared the herd, the buffalos began parting to make way for him. But not *his* buffalo. It didn't flinch or move away. It just kept staring at him with its large, dark eyes.

Sithana walked right up to it. He reached out his hand and patted the buffalo's rough, thick fur. As he did, he felt a sense of calm wash over him. For a moment, he forgot about the pain and anger he had been carrying with him for so long. He just stood there, sharing the warmth of the sun on his skin and the gentle breeze blowing through the fields with this buffalo.

Viengvilay watched from a distance, smiling as she saw the peaceful expression on Sithana's face. She knew that this was a rare moment of tranquility for him, and she hoped that he would hold onto it for as long as he could on his journey towards justice.

X

SITHANA checked the directions before getting off his motorcycle. He wanted to make sure he was at the right place. "First, turn right at the next stop onto the main road, then turn left. After about four or five blocks, you'll see the sign for Suntisuke." And there it was on the left.

Sithana opened the door to see a dance floor where loud music played and smoke clouded the ceiling. He cut through the dance floor and the crowd and headed straight for the bar. He was looking for a woman with a club foot who ran the place. He saw her sitting at the end of the bar, one boot with six inch high soles.

"I'm here to meet Mr. Tulee," Sithana told her.

She looked him up and down and then got off her stool. "Follow me," she said.

Sithana followed as she wobbled past the crowd to the wall at the end. On the right side was a dark, narrow hall-like passage leading to another building.

Tulee, a dark fat man, was sitting on a black leather couch, surrounded by young men, some of whom were passed out.

"So you're the guy, they told me about?" he said with a Hmong accent.

"That's right."

"They say you wanted something from me."

"That's right," Sithana said.

"And you're sure?"

"I am."

"And you wanted a good one, you said?"

"The best."

"Wait here," he said. He went to the back room and returned moments later, holding a brown bag. "You know these are illegal now?" he said.

"I know," Sithana said.

"You wanted the best… One strike with this can chop the neck of a bull like a kitchen knife cuts cucumbers." He reached into the bag and pulled out the machete to show Sithana.

Sithana threw down the money.

"Remember," Tulee said, as he handed Sithana the bag with the machete in it. "You and I never met."

IT was only three days now, until the US presidential visit. Sithana had made up his mind to hold the funeral on that very same day. Too much police presence, too much security and too many roadblocks and checkpoints for Touy and his men to contend with. They would be on holiday, probably even out of town as Sithana hoped.

He rode past the school, heading straight to the burial

ground. He left his motorcycle at the field, pushing it into the banana tree grove and then covered it in dry leaves. It took him about five minutes on foot to get to the burial site. He and Viengvilay had agreed to meet there to discuss the funeral.

"This is dangerous," Viengvilay said, when she saw him coming. She had heard the rustling behind her and her heart nearly jumped out of her chest. When she turned to see it was Sithana, she realized at that moment, it could have been anyone else.

"You don't have to be afraid," Sithana said. He unzipped his backpack, and pulled the machete out.

Her face turned pale.

"Where did you get that?" she asked. "And why?"

"For protection," Sithana said.

Sithana turned to his family's graves and made a deep bow.

"I can't hide anymore if we're going to hold the funeral. The preparations need to be made."

"Don't worry. Everything is ready. Your aunt has been helping. She's come to see me at the school."

"Alone?" Sithana asked.

"I don't think Ken knows… That she came to see me, I mean. She asked me if he had ever asked me about you and where you were staying. When I told him he hadn't, she said that was good, and not to tell him anything if he

ever did ask. I told her we were having the funeral the day
of the visit. She said, she would help. Then she said, she
would send some men to help, too."

"Men?" Sithana echoed.

"That's what she said. Then she told me she had to go.
She didn't want Ken to know she had been there."

"I am sorry to put everyone through this. You
especially," he said looking her in the eyes. He leaned in
to kiss her.

About an hour later, Sithana was back at his motorcycle
brushing off the dead leaves and getting ready to return to
home. The sun was already setting by the time he got on
the last ferry back; and it was night by the time he made
it back to the Panya's.

Sithana dismounted his motorcycle and took two steps
toward the house when he noticed three men lurking in
the dark by the house.

He reached into his backpack. "Who's is it?" he
shouted, holding up the machete. He heard whispering
and then laughter.

"You know how to use that?" said one voice.

"Careful. You're going to cut yourself with that…" said
another voice.

Then they all laughed again. One of them stepped
closer. "Seriously, put that away before you hurt yourself.
We're here to help. Your aunt sent us. We've been waiting

for hours. We didn't expect to run into to you in the dark."

"Yeah, we didn't mean to scare you," said the first voice.

"How can I know that you are not working for Silavong?" Sithana asked.

The one who stepped forward reached into the back of his pants and pulled out his gun. The second pulled out a machete of his own, while the third just smiled and said, "You'd be dead already."

"We're friends of your aunt. We knew your mother. Your father was a good friend of mine. We are also landowners," said the first man. "My name is Seng. This is—"

"Vanh," the second interjected. "I'm Vanh and we've had enough of these gangs stealing our land," he said. "Understand?"

"So we're to help," said the third. "I'm Akamu."

"We'll see you tomorrow morning," Vanh said, walking away. He turned around after some steps, laughing. "Oh! And bring the machete," he said.

WHEN Saturday morning arrived, Viengvilay was already busy in the kitchen preparing breakfast. Before long, Seng and Vanh appeared at the door. Seng scanned the road before entering the house.

"We can't stay here long," he told Sithana. "Akamu is

already in position waiting for us."

Viengvilay handed Vanh the bag. "Everything is ready," she said.

The room was dim, and outside was still and peaceful, with the animals grazing in the nearby field. The day that Sithana had been dreading for so long was finally here, but he felt neither vulnerable nor afraid, as he had a week ago. His mind was focused on his deceased family, especially his little sister.

Bouy stood behind Viengvilay at the entrance as the men were filing out one by one. She placed both hands on Vanh's face and gazed into his eyes, tears streaming down her cheeks. "I can see the devil in your eyes," she said. Viengvilay looked at her and then placed an arm on Sithana's shoulder. "Be careful," she said. Both women stood in the doorway watching them as they walked away and vanished into the field.

THE sun had risen, and the path leading to the burial ground had been widened, making it easier to walk. The four graves had already been dug and the remains removed. They carefully cleaned each hole, setting aside the dirt and clearing the leaves. Sithana sat between Seng and Vanh. The birds chirped and sang from all directions, but as he gazed at his family's gravesite, he was overwhelmed by a flood of emotions.

"You know, my father was Viengvilay's father's older brother," Seng told Sithana. "Viengvilay and I are cousins." Sithana was surprised. "And Vanh is my brother-in-law. I spent eight years in the army after graduating from the academy. In 1989, I was sent to the Lao-Thai border during the border dispute. I learned a lot about self-defense and execution techniques. I'm not telling you this to boast, but to let you know that we're prepared." He looked Sithana in the eyes. "Viengvilay is everything to our family. You know she is the first in the family to ever go to university?"

Seng turned away and gazed up at the towering tree. The sun shone down, casting a line of light on the fallen leaves. As the tree swayed, the light flickered on and off. They waited patiently, ready for whatever lay ahead.

IT was well past ten in the morning when the funeral got underway. Over two hundred villagers, friends, and relatives had gathered at the house to pay their respects. The sermon was in progress, with mourners gathered around the tray, heads bowed in prayer. Suddenly, the peace was shattered by the arrival of Khamhuck and his two men, roaring in on their motorcycles. They parked, guns drawn, and headed towards the house.

"Don't worry," Khamhuck said. "We're just looking for Sithana." The three of them stalked around the house, demanding that anyone who knew of Sithana's whereabouts come forward. Viengvilay sat motionless, offering no indication of rising to the occasion. Growing impatient, Khamhuck sent a child inside to summon Sithana.

"Is Sithana here?" Khamhuck asked.

"He was," Viengvilay replied matter-of-factly. "But now he's gone."

Khamhuck's eyes bulged with surprise. "The girl's got balls," he said to his two men.

"Where did he go?" Khamhuck asked.

"He's gone with the men his aunt had paid to dig out the remains. They must be there right now," she said, innocently.

Khamhuck looked around at the faces of the attendees. Was she putting him on? "Where's the burial ground?" he demanded.

"I'm not sure exactly," she replied.

A 70-year-old man stepped up. "What do you want to see the boy for?" he asked.

"Just to ask him a few questions," Khamhuck replied.

"Why are you carrying guns? Are you going to kill him?" the old man inquired.

"No, no," the three of them replied in unison.

"Come with me," the old man said, leading them to a field and pointing out the path they should follow. "You will see a very big and very tall tree. You can't miss it. You'll see a couple of boys working there," he said. As they started walking out of the village, the old man spat on the ground, cursing them to go to hell.

Viengvilay waited anxiously at the door, her eyes darting everywhere, her mouth dry, and her hands shaking. She went into the kitchen, grabbed a glass of cold water, and went back outside to stand at the door. Her friends and colleagues gathered around her, holding her hand, and together they walked out to the field, waiting to hear something from the woods.

"Trust your cousin, my dear," Bouy told her. "Seng and our boys will not let anything bad happen."

THEY could hear someone coughing in the distance. Sithana stood up and gave Seng a nudge on his back.

"Go behind the tree," Seng whispered.

Sithana scuffled off to the tree, leaning his chest against it when he reached it, watching Seng and Vanh pretending to dig a hole. Sithana saw Khamhuck walking toward them and then stop about ten feet away from Seng, standing opposite of Vanh. They were both holding long-handled shovels pretending they didn't know Khamhuck and his men were there. Behind Khamhuck was Soud, then Chur behind him. They all took their guns out and pointed them at Seng.

"Throw your shovels on the ground," Khamhuck shouted. "Listen carefully," he demanded. "Do it now or I'll blow your heads off, both of you!"

Seng chuckled to show he wasn't afraid. "You think we didn't plan for this? These holes were digging.... they're your graves!"

Vanh leaned forward, resting his crossed arms on the upright shovel, smiling. "He's got you in his sights right now. Right at your head. You so much as make a move and your head will fall before mine," Vanh added.

Khamhuck scanned the surrounding trees, but saw no one.

"You don't believe me?" Seng asked him. Seng made a gesture with his hand and a gun shot rang out from somewhere in the trees. The bullet hit the ground by Khamhuck's feet.

"My cousin," Vanh said. "We served together in the military. Expert marksman. A sniper, he is."

"You have two choices," Seng said. "Put your guns down, and we can all talk this out... or try and shoot me, and I promise, you'll never get out of this jungle alive."

Khamhuck lowered his gun and signalled his men to do the same.

"That's a smart man," Vanh said. "Throw them. To the ground... now."

The men threw their guns to the ground and moments later, Akamu emerged from the woods holding his rifle. Sithana came out from behind his tree.

Khamhuck saw them and began laughing. "So what are you going to do to us? Shovel us to death?"

"You'll never get all three of us in time," Khamhuck growled. "There's no way," he said, looking at his men.

Chur and Soud looked at each other and seemed to tense up as though they were about to leap... "No way," Khamhuck said again just as Akamu was coming up behind him, and in that moment, turned around, lunging for Akamu, grabbing for his gun and knocking him to the ground. Chur and Soud were on their man at once, with Chur going for Seng and Soud for Vanh.

Seng kicked Chur in the stomach, causing him to tumble to the ground. Vanh swung his shovel and caught Soud in the head whoe fell into the hole, Seng and Vanh had been digging. Meanwhile Sithana had gone for Khamhuck who had wrestled Akabu to the ground and was reaching for the fallen rifle next to them.

Meanwhile, Chur who had been squirming on the ground after the blow to his midriff, was now going for his own gun. Seng swung his shovel and came down hard on Chur's hand just as he was wrapping his fist around the gun. He could hear the bones crack as Chur pulled back his hand and cried out in pain. Soud, still groggy from the hit to his head was trying to climb out of the hole when Vanh walked over and kicked him hard with the back of his heel. Soud rolled back down into the hole and collapsed, unconscious. Khamhuck was on his feet, with the rifle in his hand, taking aim with his gun to shoot Akamu just as Sithana crept up behind him and hit him on the back of the head and the base of the neck. Khamhuck fell face-first into the dry leaves. Akamu grabbed the rifle. Vanh had both Khamhuck and Chur's guns now. The fight was over. They sat Khamhuck up against a tree.

SITHANA stood before Khamhuck, who was sitting on the ground looking up at Sithana and laughing. "You think you're going to get away with this?" Khamhuck asked him. "When my boss finds out what you've done, he'll come after you. He'll do a lot worse to you than what he did to your family before he does you away, you hear me?" he shouted.

Sithana put his knee on Khamhuck's chest and leaned in on it with all his weight. "So you know me? My name is Sithana," he began. "I am the second son of Mr. and Mrs. Pathavong. Liam was my older brother, and Dara was my baby sister. I loved them all very much. You're going to tell me who killed my family and why. I swear I'll—"

Suddenly a shot rang out.

Soud, who everyone had forgotten, had regained consciousness and found his gun. All they could see of him from the edge of the pit, was one hand holding a gun and another trying to grab at the dirt to pull himself out. He had shot blindly and missed. Vanh walked over and saw him crawling up the dirt, dazed and half-blind with blood coming down his skull from that first blow to his head. Vanh took up his shovel again, turned it about so that shovel's edge was facing down, and then drove it down over Soud's hand, cutting three of his fingers off.

"Okay then," Sithana said, returning his attention to Khamhuck. "If that's the way it has to be…" He reached into his backpack and pulled out the machete.

Khamhuck's face was pale. "We were only following orders," he said.

"Seeing as you're so good at following orders, you're going to follow some orders for me." Sithana put the machete to his neck. "Call your boss," he said. "Tell him you found me that you have me tied up and that I'm begging for my life."

"He won't care," Khamhuck said. "He just wants…."

"I know what he wants," Sithana interrupted. "He wants me to relinquish any inheritance I might have to my family's land and disappear from here forever."

Sithana leaned in, pressing the machete against his neck and drawing blood. "Just call him!"

Khamhuck reached into his pocket for his phone and dialed the number.

TOUY couldn't shake the feeling that something was off. His suspicion was aroused when he heard Khamhuck's voice over the phone. He had learned long ago to trust his instincts. He quickly gathered two of his men and made his way to Ken and Bouy's house, where he knew Viengvilay would be. If something was afoot, then he would be sure to secure the prize before the game even began. It was the law of the jungle, and in his mind, Touy was a lion. It was *his* jungle.

Tuoy wasn't the sort of man that believed in luck. It was simply another necessary detail that destiny would have to work for him. The day was prepared for him and the fates would free the road of obstruction. He arrived and there was already a crowd and a bustle. He was able to slip into the house with his men, with just a smile as though he were another guest. He found her in the kitchen, alone, just like that, preparing food for the funeral. "Come with me," he said, his voice cold and commanding. "Your foreigner friend has appeared and decided to sell his family property and return to Canada. I thought you might want to say goodbye."

Viengvilay knew something was wrong. She could see it in Touy's eyes, in the way his men stood behind him, poised and alert. She had no choice but to do what he said and follow him even if reluctantly, aware that something dangerous was unfolding.

They drove off, heading for the edge of Sithana's family property, where Khamhuck and Sithana were supposed to be waiting to sign the documents. Touy had his best men with him, and Viengvilay was tied up in the car. She couldn't escape even if she wanted to. The tension was palpable, and Viengvilay knew that whatever was about to happen, wouldn't end well.

AUNT Bouy had watched in horror as Viengvilay was forced into the car by Touy and his men. She knew she had to act quickly to save Viengvilay and end this terror once and for all. She ran back to the gathering at the funeral. She knew many of the elder women who had came to pay their respects at the funeral. Most of them were widows or mothers who had lost sons to these criminal gangs.

She told them what she had seen, and the women became enraged at the thought of Viengvilay being kidnapped on the day of the funeral. They knew they had to act or there would be no end to the abuse these criminals would wreak on their lives.

All at once they began marching with determination, their mourning clothes flapping in the wind. The men, and everyone at the funeral followed. They all armed themselves with sticks, bricks, and anything else they could find that could be used as a weapon. The crowd grew adding to its numbers as they marched through the village gathering more and more to their cause. Almost the entire village was behind them by the time they reached the edge of the family property, where they could see Touy and his men at a stand-off with Sithana, Seng, and Vanh. The elder women lead the charge, shouting and brandishing their weapons.

BACK at the rendez-vous spot, the sun was setting. Sithana stood at the edge of his family's property, waiting for Touy to arrive. He looked out over the vast expanse of land, the place where his family had lived and worked for generations, and felt a surge of pride mixed with sadness.

He heard the sound of a car approaching and tensed up. It was Touy, driving slowly down the dirt road, with Viengvilay tied up in the backseat. The car came to halt. Touy got out of the car, went back to pull a distraught Viengvilay out of the car. He dragged her away from the car to show her to Sithana. Sithana clenched his fists, feeling a wave of anger wash over him. He had to remain calm, he knew, to play this out carefully and not put Viengvilay in danger.

There was a smug smile on Touy's face as he held Viengvilay up by the hair. "You have what I want," he said, gesturing to the property they were standing on. "And I have what you want."

Sithana looked at him coldly. "Let her go," he said, nodding towards Viengvilay.

Touy laughed. "I don't think so. You see, I never trusted Khamhuck. I knew you were setting a trap for me, so I set one of my own."

Touy threw Viengvilay to the ground and reached for his gun to kill Khamhuck for his betrayal and for setting up the ambush. Just as Viengvilay was hitting the ground and Touy was raising the gun to aim, the crowd led by Aunt Bouy and the other elder women, suddenly burst out of the brush, brandishing weapons and chanting "leave our lands alone." Touy was caught off-guard by the surreal sight of all these elderly women descending upon them. He stood there dumb-founded by the unexpected confrontation and the villagers' show of force.

Khamhuck saw an opening and charged headfirst at Touy, knocking him to the ground. Despite having his hands tied behind his back, Khamhuck wasn't going down without a fight. Touy struggled to stand back up and draw his gun, but Khamhuck had already landed another blow.

Meanwhile, Seng and Vanh emerged from their hiding places and swiftly took down Touy's men, leaving Touy alone to face Khamhuck. Stunned and knocked down, Touy managed a last burst of strength and pushed Khamhuck off of him. He rolled to the side for his gun, and a second later was pointing it at Khamhuck. A single shot rang out, echoing through the woods. Everyone froze, unsure of what had just happened.

THE silence was broken by a cry from Viengvilay, who was still lying on the ground where Touy had thrown her. Touy had just fallen to the ground next to her, lifeless, blood flowing from his head.

Three hundred meters away, on an outcropping of rock, a federal police officer, was squinting down the barrel of his rifle. Moments later a convoy of federal policemen and what looked like CIA agents to Sithana, appeared on the scene. They had heard the commotion and saw the mob of villagers led by the elder women marching into the jungle and followed to investigate. Helicopters were heard overhead as the officers assessed the situation.

Sithana ran to Viengvilay's side, helping her to sit up. Holding her, he raised his hand and declared, "I am Canadian! And this is my fiancée." He leaned in and kissed Viengvilay deeply.

The federal police officer eyed Sithana suspiciously, but lowered his rifle. The other officers soon followed suit, and the CIA men began to confer amongst themselves. The villagers watched as the officers secured the area and began tending to the injured and restoring order.

Meanwhile, Khamhuck was being arrested. Touy was lying dead, with a small pool of blood forming around him.

In the background, Sithana and Viengvilay embrace, tears on their cheeks. They had won. They had come through. There was nothing but a clear path ahead of them.